Mail Order Miracle

Kirsten Osbourne

Brides of Beckham

Francine "Frankie" Weston is an independent woman. She moved to Idaho to homestead with her older brother at the tender age of seventeen, pretending to be a man. Now, at twenty, she's ready to marry, but she doesn't want to admit she's deceived everyone, so she sends for a mail order groom—one who's willing to take her last name. She doesn't think it's possible, but she's willing to wait for just the right man to make her happy.

Wallace Miller, a former member of the demon horde, feels like his life is going nowhere. His reputation as a troublemaker has followed him into adulthood, and he can't seem to catch a break. When his older sister, Elizabeth, shows him a letter from a woman wanting a man to marry, he's shocked before he sees the potential of the situation. Meeting his pants-wearing independent bride comes as a bit of a shock. Will the two of them be able to come to a compromise about how a lady should act? Or will they be destined to be partners in life, but never partners in love?

Acknowledgements:

This book will tie together two series. You will recognize characters from the Brides of Beckham series, but you will be introduced to a beautiful locale in Idaho, called River's End Ranch. River's End Ranch is a series of books (contemporary) I'm writing with four close friends.

I've included the first chapter of book eight in the series (the most recent release) so you can get a feel for that series as well. I hope you'll give it a try! The first book in the series is Short-Order Sheriff, about one of Frankie and Wally's descendants, who finds love on the very same ranch talked about in this story.

I hope you enjoy, and Merry Christmas! Have a very happy 2017.

Much love,

Kirsten

Chapter One

River's End Ranch, Riston, Idaho 1892

Frankie Weston leaned back, rocking the old wooden chair on its back legs. "I've decided I need to get married. I'm sick of doing double work around here. We need help."

Frankie's brother, Willard, frowned. "What do you mean? How are you going to make that work?"

Frankie shrugged. "Same way anyone else does, I guess. Hard work, patience, and a whole lot of praying."

"But...how do you think you're going to find someone? It's not like you can go to a barn dance or an ice cream social to find a mate."

"Haven't you ever heard of mail order brides?" Frankie asked. "I found a little matchmaker that sends out brides to men in need."

"But...how's that going to help?" Willard asked, obviously perplexed.

Frankie leaned forward, palms on the table. "I'm going to ask for a mail order groom. Why not? It's possible, right?"

Willard sighed, shaking his head. "You've lost it, Frankie. By the way, we got a letter from Ma when I rode to town today. She said you need to wear a skirt."

Frankie wrinkled her nose. "How can I do a man's work if I'm wearing a skirt? That's why I need a husband. I'm ready to wear skirts again, but you can't do all the ranch chores by yourself. Not with two homesteads!"

"I guess."

The siblings had decided to move West from New York together, and Francine had become Frankie. Her real name was on the documents, of course, but she hadn't wanted to draw undue attention to herself, so she'd started dressing as a man and answering to a man's name. Thankfully the nickname had been one she'd had as a child, and she was used to it. After three years of doing a man's job, she was ready to stay in the house all day and cook and clean. Women's work sounded downright glorious! Especially since she'd been doing women's work *and* men's work.

Frankie shrugged. "I'm going to write a letter tonight, and I need you to take it to town in the morning. If providence is on our side, I'll have a husband before winter."

"Are you going to ask for someone who doesn't mind a woman who wears britches most of the time?"

She nodded. "Definitely. Of course, once he gets here, I'll be able to wear skirts again. I'm also going to ask for a man who is willing to change his last name to Weston. I know it's strange, but I like the whole spread being one ranch, and I want my kids being raised with the Weston name."

Willard laughed, shaking his head at his sister. "You're never going to find a man willing to give up his name. Have you lost your ever-loving mind?"

"I admit it won't be easy. Why—it'll take a mail order miracle."

"You write your letter, and I'll send it."

"I'll write it while you do the dishes," Frankie insisted. "I've done them every night this week after spending every day mending fences with you. It's your turn!"

Willard grumbled, but he got to his feet and cleared the table.

Frankie got up and got some paper and a pencil, quickly scrawling out a letter. Once she was done, she read over it. "It's not going to get any better than that."

Willard just shook his head.

*****

Beckham, Massachusetts

Wally Miller swiped his hand over his head, wiping away the sweat. It was an unusually balmy October in Beckham, Massachusetts. He was working for the mercantile in town doing deliveries, and he was daydreaming about going West. He was always daydreaming about going West. He loved the idea of disappearing and changing his identity. He'd been a member of the "demon horde" as a child, and no one wanted to give him work. No man wanted to let Wally court his daughter. It was enough to make a man just take off and tell no one where he was going.

Of course, to do that, he'd need to have enough money saved up to make it work. And where would he go? He was working for the mercantile on a trial basis. He saved every dime he made, but it never seemed to be enough.

He unhitched the horses and took them to the livery, glad his shift was over. As he handed over the horses and left to walk home to the farm where he lived with his parents and three thousand siblings—okay, there were really only ten still at home—he saw his older sister's butler. He shook his head. Even after six years, he couldn't get used to Elizabeth having a butler.

"Wallace, your sister would like to see you."

Wally raised an eyebrow. He wanted to make a snide remark about her highness, but he wouldn't. Bernard the butler was actually kind of scary. He was the kind of man that seemed nice and kind, but could kill you with one hand tied behind his back. Wally wasn't sure why he thought that about him, but he did. He nodded. "Sure. I'll head on over."

Bernard fell into step beside Wally. "I'll drive you home when you're finished."

"I can walk. What does Lizard Breath want with me anyway?" When the old nickname slipped out, he bit his lip, wondering if the butler would be angry with him.

"Miss Miller didn't tell me."

Wally thought he saw the corner of the older man's mouth quirk, but he couldn't be sure. *Stodgy old goat.* "I'm sure it's something of global importance."

When the butler didn't respond, Wally remained silent for the rest of the short walk. He didn't want to get onto Bernard's bad side anyway.

He was led down the hallway to the room at the very end of the hall on the left, and he saw his sister sitting quietly at a desk, her hand poised as she wrote a note to someone. "Hey, sis."

Elizabeth put down her pencil and hurried to Wally, hugging him tightly. "Thanks for coming. I have a proposition for you. Won't you sit down?"

As Wally sat on the sofa, she asked Bernard for tea and cookies to be served. "Do you need something more substantial than cookies?"

He nodded. "I'd love something more substantial than cookies."

Elizabeth rolled her eyes. "We'll have one extra for dinner tonight, Bernard."

Wally grinned as Bernard nodded and slipped away. The food was much better at Elizabeth's house than it was at his parents' house. She had a cook and money. Their parents barely scraped by. He was going to take advantage while he could. "What's going on, Lizard?" The old nickname popped out before he could think about it, and she grinned in response.

"I received a letter today that I think might interest you."

He frowned. Elizabeth was a mail order bride broker. She matched up lonely women in Beckham to lonely men in the West. Why would he be interested in one of her letters? "Really?"

She sorted through a stack of letters on her desk and handed him one, watching him as he read it.

Dear Proprietor of the Beckham Mail Order Bride Organization,

This letter will probably seem odd to you, but I do hope you'll be able to help me. Let me tell you a bit about myself. I'm a twenty-year-old woman, who moved to Idaho with my brother three years ago. I will confess that I lied about my age so that I could have my own homestead.

When I moved here, I was well aware that the unmarried women of the area would be far outnumbered by the bachelors, so I chose to disguise myself as a man. I had my brother start calling me "Frankie" instead of Francine, and I wore britches instead of skirts. I've been doing a man's work for far too long, and I'm ready to marry, but I don't think any of the men in the area will have me after thinking of me as a man for so long.

Here's where you enter the picture. I would like you to send me a mail order groom. I don't even know if such a thing exists, but if not, it should for women like me. I would like a man between the ages of twenty-one and thirty-five. I would like his name to start with a W or that he be willing to change his name to one that starts with a W, as all men in my family have W names. The most important part of my request comes next—I would like him to forgo his surname and take on my last name, which is Weston. I want my children and their children to inherit the land that I've plowed with my own hands, but I want them to have the Weston name.

I realize what I'm asking for is a very tall order, and I will certainly understand if it can't be done. Please forward any correspondence of candidates to me here at River's End Ranch in Riston, Idaho. My brother and I will gladly pay the way for a man to ride the train West to join us here.

I look forward to hearing your response.

Francine (Frankie) Weston

Wally blinked a few times, finally looking up and meeting Elizabeth's gaze. Her green eyes were very like his own, but his hair was darker, a medium brown instead of blond like hers. "I don't know what to say."

Elizabeth smiled. "I knew you'd be startled, but I think you'd make a good candidate. There you'd be starting anew. No one would know about the demon horde. You'd have a place of your own to share with a woman. I would bet she's tall and masculine to have been able to pull off being a man for so long, but you're a tall man. I don't know if that would matter to you."

"But—give up my name? How could I do that?"

"Only your last name. Women do it when they marry, and I see nothing wrong with a man doing it for a woman. Especially a woman who is willing to help him make his dream of having a cattle ranch in the West come true. Think about it, Wally. They've named the ranch River's End. Doesn't that sound like a beautiful place to live?"

"It does. My head is reeling. When do I need to have an answer by?"

Elizabeth shrugged. "You know as much as I do. I'll give you a week to make a decision before I start looking for another groom for her. That should give you sufficient time to make up your mind. Don't you think?"

"I guess so." He leaned back on the sofa, the letter still clutched in his hand. Frankie. Could he marry a woman named Frankie? He didn't know. He thought about Alice Weist, the girl who lived on the next farm over from his parents'. He'd asked her father if he could court her, and the man had laughed in his face. He'd been finished with school for four years and had just recently found someone who would give him a chance at working, but he was constantly watched. He'd never dreamed his childhood pranks would be so hard to live down as an adult.

"You don't have to make a decision now, Wally," Elizabeth said gently, her face as sweet as ever.

"I think I already have. I'm going to do it." As soon as he'd said the words, he knew they were the right answer. "And I'm not doing this writing back and forth thing. I have a little money. I'm going to take the next train to Idaho."

She blinked at him a couple of times before throwing her head back to laugh. "You never did anything the easy way! Do you have proper clothes? Are you sure you have enough money?"

He shrugged. "I don't know what a train ticket to Idaho costs, but I'm going to find out." He jumped to his feet, pacing back and forth. "Do you think this man-woman will start wearing skirts when I get there? Or will she keep wearing britches? I don't want anyone to think I'm married to a man."

Elizabeth grinned. "I think she's ready to admit she's a woman or she wouldn't be looking for a husband. And I wouldn't start thinking of her as a man-woman, or that's going to come out of your mouth once you're together, and she's going to put you on a train right back to Massachusetts."

"Do you think Ma and Pa will be mad if I do this?"

"No, I don't. They didn't have a problem with Susan becoming a mail order bride, and she was a woman. They won't worry as much about you."

He nodded. "That's true. And they were fine with Charlie staying in Montana when she went out there as a traveling companion. I guess we'll find out, though, won't we?"

"We will."

After dinner, Bernard drove him home, and he said little. He was so busy thinking about his future that he couldn't even find the energy to annoy the serious man. When they got to the farm, he jumped down. "Thanks for the ride."

He hurried into the house and found his parents together in the parlor, ignoring the massive amounts of chaos around them. The older girls took care of the younger children, which had always been the way in their home. There was writing on the walls, and dirt on the floors. His mother tried to keep up, but she refused to discipline her children which made the whole effort pointless.

His mother looked up from her mending when he entered the room. "You weren't here for supper."

"I ate with Elizabeth in town."

His mom frowned at him. "With Elizabeth? I didn't know you were going to see her."

"She sent for me today. She got a letter from a woman wanting a mail order groom, and I'm going to do it. I'm going to Idaho to marry a stranger."

His father grinned at him. "You've been wanting to go West. Do it, son."

Wally smiled. "I plan on it. And I'm not waiting for her to send me a train ticket either. I've saved my wages from the past couple of weeks, and I'm going to take off as soon as I can get a ticket."

"Does she even know you're coming?" his mother asked with a frown.

He shook his head. "Nope. She'll be surprised, won't she? I'm going upstairs to pack. Hopefully you'll be able to move Mikey up to my bed tomorrow night." Mikey was the second youngest of the Miller children his mother kept popping out. He thought she may be done, because it had been a couple of years since Rebekah was born, and she didn't seem to be pregnant yet.

His mother shrugged. "It would be nice to be down to only one baby in our room. Make sure you write and tell us that you made it safe. I don't trust those trains. They go too fast!"

Having received all the blessings he knew he would from his parents, he hurried up the stairs to throw all of his belongings into a carpet bag. He didn't have much, but he didn't need much. He was going to Idaho to marry a stranger who wasn't even expecting him.

From drudgery to excitement in one day. He couldn't wait to be on that train!

Chapter Two

Wally was on the train shortly after noon the following day. The mercantile owner hadn't been terribly upset—or surprised. He hadn't expected to have a long-time worker who had been a member of the demon horde. His reaction made Wally realize he'd made the right decision. He needed to be with people who had no preconceived notions of who he was or what he was about.

The train trip would be long and tedious, and he'd have two hours in a stage coach once he'd arrived. Of course, after that, there was no telling how long it would take to find River's End Ranch. Hopefully the people in town would know it.

He had never been on a train and watched excitedly as they pulled out of the station. He'd never even been as far away as Boston! Even if things didn't work out with Frankie, he'd have the adventure of a lifetime!

*****

Frankie wiped the sweat from her forehead. The house was hot. She was canning pickles today. It was one of her least favorite tasks, but it needed to be done, so she'd do it. Willard was on the ranch, cutting firewood for the long winter they knew would hit any day. It was early November, and they hadn't had a good, hard snowfall yet, but it would be coming any day, she was sure.

As she was setting the jars on the counter to cool, she heard a knock on the door. Wiping her hands on a towel, she grabbed a hat from a hook, and tucked her long braid under it. She'd taken to working in britches even in the house, but she did have to hide her waist-length blond hair if anyone came along. She picked up a pistol from the work table where she kept one loaded and ready, tucking it into the waistband at the base of her spine.

She opened the door wide and found herself staring at a handsome stranger. "May I help you?" she asked in her gruffest voice. She rarely left the ranch, because she didn't want to be found out, but when someone came along, she was made sure she was always ready to deal with them. Sometimes neighbors needed help, but this was no neighbor.

"Yes, I'm looking for Frankie Weston." The man had a carpet bag beside him, and looked rumpled, almost as if it had been several days since he'd slept.

Why is someone looking for me? "I'm Frankie." As she looked at him, she wished she was wearing a fancy dress and elbow length gloves, ready to dance the night away, instead of wearing britches, an old apron, and a worn work shirt, with her breasts bound beneath it.

He looked at her for a moment as if he could see right through her disguise to the woman within. She gave a slight shudder, hoping she was wrong, while also hoping she was right! She was so confused! She wanted her disguise to be good enough no one would see through, but she also wanted him to see her as a woman. "I'm Wallace Miller. I'm your mail order groom."

"My—" Frankie wasn't often struck dumb, but at that moment, she wasn't sure she'd ever find words again. "I—I thought I'd receive a letter before you left Massachusetts." What was he doing here? She'd meant to greet her future husband properly—in a dress!

Wallace shrugged. "May I come in?"

"I don't know..."

He sighed. "I'm dead tired. If it makes you feel better, leave the door wide open. Get a gun. I don't care. I just need to sit for a bit." He understood that she may be worried about allowing a stranger into her home, but he needed to sit down somewhere. He'd gotten a ride to about a mile from their home, and then he'd had to walk from there. He didn't mind long walks, but his body was so tired from the train ride. He felt like he could still feel the thing rumbling beneath him.

Frankie looked at the clock on the fireplace mantle and knew that Willard would be there within a few minutes. She'd leave the door open—and cool off in the process. What could it hurt?

She opened the door wide for him to enter. "My brother will be here in just a few minutes."

Wally nodded, walking into the house and collapsing into one of the chairs at her table. "Usually you would have received a letter before I left home, but I didn't want to wait that long. I'm ready to start a new life in the West, and I'm here to do that. Just as soon as I sleep for a day or two." He hid a yawn behind his huge hand.

"I wish I'd known." She stood awkwardly for a moment, before she returned to work. He'd been rude enough to show up unannounced, so she could continue to work in front of him. She had no choice anyway. "I'm just making a simple supper tonight. I've been canning all day and haven't had time to prepare anything."

"I don't mind simple meals." He watched her as she lifted a door in the floor and descended into the cellar, coming back up a minute later with potatoes held in her apron. He couldn't help but wonder how anyone could mistake her for a man with mannerisms like that. A man would have looked for a bucket to carry potatoes. A woman carried them in an apron.

"Tell me about yourself," she said, washing the potatoes with water she pumped in. She efficiently peeled them and cut them into small pieces for frying.

As he watched her, he saw definite advantages to women wearing pants. He could see her bottom outlined very well. She didn't look a bit like a man to him. "I was raised in a family of fifteen children. We were referred to as the 'demon horde' because we spent all of our time playing tricks on people. Teachers never lasted more than a month or two, because we'd scare them all away." He wasn't sure why he was telling her this. Hadn't he moved to Idaho to avoid the reputation he'd created for himself back East? "My dream has always been to come out

West to ranch, but I didn't think I'd ever be able to save enough. Not many people in town wanted to hire me because of my reputation."

Frankie nodded. She could see their concerns. The words 'demon horde' didn't make her want to marry him either! "I see."

"My older sister, Elizabeth, runs the mail order bride agency you wrote to. When she saw your letter, she immediately thought of me. I was supposed to write you back and go through all the regular channels, but...I was in a hurry. I'm sorry if I've put you out by my unexpected arrival."

She considered telling him it was fine, but that would have been a lie. "I'm sure my brother will be happy to have someone here to help him so quickly. I try hard with the ranch chores, but I'm just not strong enough for some things." She cut off several pieces of bacon and put them on to fry. "How'd you find us?"

"You said in your letter you were near Riston, Idaho. I took a train, and then a stagecoach, and a nice man gave me a ride from town."

"Did you tell him you were here to marry me?" she asked, alarm in her face.

He shook his head. "No, that's your secret. I told him I came here to work, which is the truth, just not all of it."

She dried her hands on a towel and turned to look at him. "Since you came unannounced, and I really had no time to prepare myself, how would you feel about staying with my brother for a week or two, and we can get to know each other before we decide if we really want to marry or not?"

He shrugged. "I can deal with that. Is there room?"

She blushed. "There's not room here. You'll stay with my brother."

"Oh, I guess I just assumed you lived together."

"We would, but part of the rules of homesteading is we have to build up each of the plots of land, so he has a cabin, and I have the proper house. He doesn't even have a kitchen, because we eat all meals here."

"Will he mind?"

Frankie shrugged. "He's pretty affable. I don't think he'll mind at all."

There was a stomping outside the door and Willard stepped into the room, looking around. "Who're you?" By the look on his face, it was clear that he wasn't used to coming in from work to find his sister with a man.

Wally got to his feet. "Wallace Miller. I came from Massachusetts to marry your sister."

Willard grinned. "I guess we got our mail order miracle, huh Frankie?"

Frankie wrinkled her nose at him, and Wally stared. How could anyone believe she was a man? She was a petite little thing. "I guess so. He's going to stay with you for a couple of weeks while we decide if we'll suit."

"I'm not sure that's how it's supposed to work. Aren't you supposed to marry him as soon as he gets here?" Willard asked, removing his hat and scratching his head.

Frankie shrugged. "That's how it would have worked if I'd known he was coming. I'm not prepared to marry yet. I need to make myself a dress." Her old dresses were much too small. She hadn't really gained weight since moving to Idaho, but she'd gained a great deal of muscles, which made the dresses very snug.

Wally sighed. "I was worried you'd keep wearing britches after we married and people would think I was married to a man." He was very relieved to find out that wasn't her plan.

She blushed, turning away. "Not at all. I just have to figure out how I'm going to admit that I'm really a woman." She realized then she was still wearing her cowboy hat, and she plucked it off her head and hung it on the hook on the wall, her long braid falling out and hanging down her back.

Wally stared at her. "Your hair is pretty."

What a way with words the man had. She wasn't sure he was the man she'd waited her whole life for by any means. "Wash up. I'll have supper on the table in a minute."

Both men washed up, and Wally took the chair Willard indicated. Frankie served them both generous helpings of eggs, bacon, and fried potatoes. "Coffee or milk?" she asked.

"Coffee if you have it," Wally responded immediately. He wouldn't be able to stay awake through supper without a little coffee in his system. It had been a very long journey.

Frankie poured coffee for him and for her brother, but she poured a glass of milk for herself. She took her place at the table, and bowed her head while Willard prayed for them.

Wally took one bite of her cooking and sighed contentedly. "You're a good cook," he said, surprise in his voice.

"Why do you sound so shocked?" Frankie asked. Did he think she knew nothing of being a woman because she pretended to be a man?

"I guess I thought that you liked acting like a man so much that you never really learned to be a woman."

She sighed. "I was raised in Upstate New York. My mother taught me to be a proper young lady. I didn't even tell her I was running around in pants, but big brother here couldn't keep his mouth shut. So now Mother knows, and she's not exactly pleased with me. Every time she sends a letter, she tells me to put on a skirt, which I will happily do as soon as I'm ready to get married."

"So why pretend to be a man at all?"

She shrugged. "I never planned to. I had a couple of pairs of pants with me, which I knew I'd need to wear to do some of the hard work here, but when we were in that town getting ready to go to the survey office to choose our claims, it was a loud, rough crowd there. I had four men proposition me in the space of ten minutes when we first got to town, and I thought I'd be safer pretending to be a man. And I have been." She'd missed female companionship, though. It was hard to be a man all the time. Only her brother knew the truth, and now this man.

Willard looked at Wally. "Have you ever worked on a ranch?"

Wally shook his head. "Nope. I grew up on a farm, and I've spent a lot of time working for my pa since I finished school, so I know farm chores, and ranch chores can't be that much different."

Willard shrugged. "I guess we'll see. You plan on working with me tomorrow?"

Wally thought about how tired he was and how good it would feel to sleep late the following morning, but he nodded his head. "I'm up for work whenever I'm needed."

"Good. We get up at five in the morning. If Frankie can stay in and cook and clean and act like a girl most of the time, she'll be pretty darn happy."

"I'll have breakfast ready at half past five." She loved the idea of not having to go out and use her muscles. Maybe she could get some sewing done the next day. She wasn't sure she wanted to marry Wally, but she knew she wanted to marry someone. Maybe it would be him.

Wally nodded. "I'm going to have to head to bed right after supper then, I'm afraid. I'm pretty tired from all that traveling."

Frankie nodded. "Do you want me to heat some water for a bath before you head over to Willard's place?"

"I'm too tired to take a bath. I'd drown." He knew he smelled bad, but he just needed sleep more than he needed to be clean. He'd bathe tomorrow.

After supper, Willard stood. "I'll take care of the dishes tonight. You walk Wallace to my house and make up a bed for him."

Frankie nodded. There were two beds in Willard's cabin, because they took on a ranch hand from time to time. There was simply too much work for two people. She'd still be helping on the ranch on occasion, but at least she could stay inside the majority of the time.

She took one of the lanterns from the wall and held it up for him, and he noticed that the sun had set. Now when had that happened? He followed her down the steps and outside, breathing deeply of the fresh air. "This is a beautiful piece of land, Miss Weston."

"Please, call me Francine."

"Francine? Is that what you go by?"

She shrugged. "I did when I was back East. Willard has gotten into the bad habit of calling me Frankie, but I still think of myself as Francine most of the time."

"I go by Wally," he told her.

"Wally? That suits you better than Wallace."

"Oh? Why is that?"

"Wallace seems like an old man with a pipe. You're too young to be a Wallace."

"You're too pretty to be a Frankie," he countered, watching as she stumbled at his words.

"You can't call me pretty. I know that I don't look like a woman in these old clothes." As she said it, she realized she wanted him to see her in a dress. She wanted him to know there was so much more to her than what he saw before him. She'd be sewing like crazy.

"I can't believe anyone ever thought you were a man, Francine. I looked at you and knew immediately."

"Only because you knew to look. No one else has known in the three years we've been here." Of course, she didn't exactly go to church every week. She mostly stayed on the ranch. Only when someone came out to help them with something did they see her.

"I'd have known. I promise you I would."

She opened the door to Willard's cabin and hurried over to make up the extra bed. "I think you'll be quite comfortable," she said softly. "Goodnight, Wally."

"Goodnight, Francine." He watched her leave, a smile on his lips. She was beautiful, and there was nothing masculine about her.

Tomorrow, when he didn't smell quite so bad, he'd take her for a walk and try to steal a kiss.

Chapter Three

Early the next morning, Frankie was setting a plate of pancakes on the table to join the pile of bacon on another plate, when Wally and Willard came into the house, both of them shedding their coats and hanging them on a hook. "It's getting cold out there," Willard told her, rubbing his hands together briskly.

Frankie poured all three of them some coffee and sat at the table, waiting for them to join her. "How did you sleep?" she asked Wally. She'd wanted to wait until he spoke to her first, because she felt that was polite, but also he was her house guest, in a way, so she felt like she should be a good hostess. She couldn't figure out which rules of politeness to apply!

"Like a log." Wally glanced at Willard. "I hope I didn't keep you awake with my snores."

Willard shook his head. "After a hard day of work here at the ranch, I don't think being trampled by my own herd would have woken me up."

"Good. I didn't want to give my host a sleepless night the first time we slept in the same house." Wally grinned. "Does Frankie snore?"

Willard laughed softly. "That's not something an intelligent man would ever answer about the woman who cooks his food."

Frankie smiled at Wally, her heart pounding faster as she thought about what he might mean to her. "My brother enjoys food that's not burned or poisoned."

Wally nodded. "He is indeed a smart man, Francine."

"I know he is." She secretly marveled that he was calling her Francine. Maybe he didn't use her given name often, but he used it often enough that she felt a flutter in her tummy from it. "What are you planning on doing today?"

"Whatever your brother tells me to do!"

Willard ate a bite of his pancakes, looking at Wally. "How are you with a rifle?"

Wally shrugged. "I did some rabbit hunting at home and hit my mark most of the time. Why?"

"We have some deer that have been moving in too close on our property. We'll need to take care of them." Willard smiled. "Frankie makes the best venison stew you ever tasted. If we can get one home and hang it from a tree before lunch, I bet she'll make stew for supper."

Frankie smiled. "I will. But you'd better hurry." She ate the last of her breakfast and carried her plate to the sink, immediately heating water for the dishes. "Would either of you care for another cup of coffee?"

Wally nodded. The truth was he had slept well, but it hadn't been nearly enough. He'd slept very little on the journey from Massachusetts, because the train had been so crowded. Now that he'd reached his destination, he wanted to sleep for a couple of days, but he wasn't about to be thought of as a slacker to the brother and sister. "I'd love another."

She carried the pot over and poured him another cup. "We'll heat you up some bathwater after supper."

He wrinkled his nose. He knew he smelled badly, but there was little he could do about it. He'd washed earlier before coming over, but he needed a real bath. "That would be nice, as long as it's not too much trouble."

Frankie bit back her reply. She'd started to tell him that the trouble was worth lack of agony to her nostrils, but that was something she said to her brother, not her potential husband. How he did working for Willard would go a long way toward whether or not she'd marry him. "I'd be happy to do it."

After Wally finished his second cup of coffee, the two men were off. "We'll be here for lunch!" Willard called over his shoulder as they left.

"Bring me back some venison!" she told him, starting to work on the breakfast dishes. As soon as she'd finished that, she scrubbed her kitchen, started a soup for lunch, and mixed up enough dough to make a few loaves of bread, leaving it to rise on the work table.

When she'd finally finished all that, she sat down with a length of fabric her brother had gone clear to Post Falls to purchase for her. It was a pretty pink calico with tiny little flowers, and she traced her fingers over it. She loved the idea of having a pretty dress to wear for her wedding. She would probably still have to wear her britches a lot, because they were easier to work in, but she would have something nice for when she wanted to feel like a lady.

She made quick, decisive cuts with her pattern, and then she began sewing. She'd used a sewing machine back in New York, but all her clothes had been purchased since they'd moved to Idaho, so it was slow going at first, but she gradually gained speed. She stopped once to punch down the bread, but sat right back down to work on the dress.

Shortly before noon, she heard the men outside. Peeking out the window, she saw them stringing a buck from an old oak tree, and she smiled. Venison stew for supper would be a reality.

Quickly hiding the dress she was working on in her bedroom, she popped the loaves of bread into the oven. The men would take a little while to deal with the deer, and she would have lunch ready when they came in. By the time lunch was over, the deer would have bled out enough that they could bring a big enough piece for her to make into stew that evening. She looked forward to some meals with venison. It felt like she used pork for almost everything.

She was just sliding the loaves of bread out of the oven when the two men came in. "Wash your hands!"

They both washed their hands obediently. "Wally shot the buck," Willard informed her. "I'm not sure I could have gotten it from that distance, but he did it with one shot."

Frankie smiled at Wally. "Thank you."

He felt himself lost in her eyes. Even in britches, she was the prettiest girl he'd ever met. "My pleasure."

He sat down at the table and waited as she put a bowl of soup in front of him.

"Do you want coffee? Or water?" She usually served water with lunch, but she'd noticed he seemed to prefer coffee with every meal.

"I'll have coffee," Wally told her. "Will we hunt more after lunch?"

Willard shook his head. "We'll wait until most of this meat is gone and get another. I'd like to get more of them away from the ranch faster, but I'm not willing to waste the meat."

"Have you thought about selling some in town?"

Willard shrugged. "I guess we could. I hadn't thought about it much. We need to remove a few tree stumps today. I want to clear an area for Frankie to put in a kitchen garden this spring. She's wanted one since we've moved here, but there's been no time with everything else we do. This coming spring, she'll have one."

"All right," Wally responded. He had no idea what removing stumps entailed, but if Willard was willing to show him, then he was willing to do the job. He would do anything to prove he was worthy to marry the woman who was cooking for them.

She set a plate of sliced bread on the table, along with a ball of butter. Then she took her place across from Willard, with Wally sitting at the foot of the table.

"You making me some venison stew for supper?" Willard asked, taking a big bite of the soup in front of him.

"Of course I am. How could I not make my brother his favorite meal?"

Wally watched the byplay between them, feeling like an outsider. "I can't wait to taste your stew," he said softly.

She smiled at him, making his insides flutter. "What's your favorite meal, Wally?"

"I'm particularly fond of chicken and dumplings and roast beef. It depends on the day of the week which is my favorite." Wally spooned up a bite of the potato soup she'd served. "This is really good!"

"You always seem so surprised when I cook something well." Frankie shook her head at him. "I keep telling you that I was raised properly."

"It just seems strange that someone wearing pants is a good cook."

"Plenty of men cook." Frankie knew she was being persnickety, but at the moment she didn't care. He seemed to think that the ability to cook went hand in hand with wearing a skirt, and she didn't like it.

"I didn't mean to offend you." Wally had never courted a woman, though he'd wanted to. Learning the fine nuances of saying the right thing was going to take him a while, and he knew it. He only hoped the pretty girl beside him would understand that. "I was trying to pay you a compliment, but it came out wrong."

She sighed. "I knew you were being complimentary, and I took it wrong anyway. I'm sorry." She hated to admit she was wrong and apologize, but she tried to do it when it was called for.

Willard looked back and forth between his two table companions. "You two are already bickering like an old married couple. Might as well tie the knot soon."

Frankie glared at her brother. "I don't think this discussion concerns you, Willard."

"Maybe not, but if you're going to argue in front of me, you'll be getting my opinion on the matter."

Wally sighed. He hadn't meant to bicker at all. Had she taken a dislike to him? Maybe after he'd bathed and put on the last of his clean-smelling clothes, she'd like him better. It was Saturday. He hoped they'd not work on Sunday, so he could wash his clothes, now that he thought about it. "What do we do on Sundays around here?"

Frankie frowned. “I couldn’t deal with going to church and pretending to be a man, so Willard and I worship at home. You’re welcome to join us or go into town to the church there.”

“I’ll worship with you.” He didn’t have any desire to be away from her. His goal was to get to know her better. “Do we work on Sundays?”

“No more than absolutely necessary. I cook, we gather eggs, and milk the cows. I wash up the dishes.”

“Would it be a problem if I washed my laundry tomorrow?” He’d never done laundry, of course, because men didn’t do that, but he couldn’t ask her to wash his clothes until after they were married.

“Willard brings his dirty clothes over on Monday mornings, and I wash them. Make sure yours are here and I’ll get them done.” It wouldn’t be warm enough to hang the clothes out for much longer without them freezing on the line. She’d need to start hanging them in the basement.

“Are you sure you don’t mind?” Wally asked, surprised that she offered so readily.

She shook her head. “Of course not. It’s easy enough for me to wash them when I’m doing ours.” Besides, if she was going to marry him, she’d be washing his clothes for a lot of years to come.

After the men left, she quickly cut up the venison they brought to her and browned it for stew. She chopped up onions, potatoes, and carrots and added them, before washing up the lunch dishes.

It wasn’t long before she was once again seated in her rocking chair in the corner of the room, sewing as quickly as her fingers would allow. She wanted the dress done soon, so they could go into town to marry. She’d decided she’d have him, if only he’d ask her. She knew it was somewhat of a hasty decision, but when she looked at him, she felt flutters in her tummy and her heart beat faster. Never before had she reacted that way to a man. Yes, she’d marry him. She knew him well enough.

*****

Wally wiped the sweat off his brow. "So how long do I need to wait to ask Francine if she'll marry me?"

Willard leaned forward on his shovel. "Francine? You going to call her by her real name?"

"I can't ask a man to marry me." Wally hated that people called her Frankie. He hated that people believed she was a man. He wouldn't add to it.

"I reckon a couple of days is enough. Why, if it were me, I'd probably ask her tonight. You've had three of her meals, so you know she can cook. She's watched you eat three meals, so she knows you don't talk with your mouth full or throw peas at the supper table. Ask her."

"Really? I thought she'd want me to wait a month or two."

Willard laughed. "Frankie? That woman is the most impetuous girl in the whole nation. No, you ask her tonight, and I guarantee, she's already decided what she's going to say."

Wally got back to work, thinking about Willard's words. If she'd already made her mind up, there was no reason to wait, was there?

Chapter Four

The stew was everything Wally had been led to believe and more. He considered dropping to one knee and proposing right there at the table, but he knew she wouldn't accept a proposal from a man who was as filthy as he was. When supper was over, he helped carry in the bathtub and added the water Frankie had set on the stove to boil before they sat down to eat.

The tub had been placed in her bedroom. He felt strange being in her room, even though she wasn't there, because it was private. It was the only room in her house that Willard didn't seem to think he had the right to do whatever he wanted in.

As soon as Wally was out of the way, Frankie heated another large pan of water to do the dishes. Keeping her voice low, she asked, "How'd he do today?"

Willard tipped his chair back onto two legs as he studied his sister. "He's a hard worker. Doesn't talk a whole lot, but I think that's in his favor."

Frankie nodded once. "I can agree with that. I think I'm going to marry him if he asks."

"I figured you were leaning in that direction. Your venison stew has never been better."

"If I spend some time sewing my dress tomorrow, I can have it ready to wear by Tuesday afternoon. Would that be too soon to marry? Do you think?"

"I don't think so. Are you sure that's what you want?"

Frankie couldn't mention the flutters in her belly when she looked at Wally. Not with her brother. "If he's a good worker, then that's what we need around here."

Willard studied her before finally nodded. "I just want you to be happy."

"You know I wouldn't do anything that would make me unhappy. I'm not that self-sacrificing."

"You should probably suggest a walk after his bath then. Spend a little time alone with him."

Frankie nodded. She could do that. It even made sense. "You wouldn't mind?"

He shook his head. "I think we'll both have to get used to the idea we won't spend nearly as much time together if you're married. You'll be off doing married stuff, and I'll still be in my lonely bachelor cabin."

She frowned. "You'll still take meals with us. I won't have you trying to figure out how to cook over a fire in that tiny cabin of yours."

Willard nodded. "I think I'll need to. Besides, we're partners, not just siblings. River's End Ranch belongs to both of us."

Wally emerged then in clean clothes, his hair freshly combed. He felt funny, knowing he looked much better than he had since he'd met Frankie. "Would you care to walk with me, Francine?"

Frankie nodded, walking to get her coat off the hook on the wall beside the door. Soon, she'd be able to admit she was a woman and hang her shawl there, wearing that for walks. For now, she couldn't risk being spotted from the road.

He held her coat for her, something no man had done since they'd left New York. It felt awkward, but she thanked him. She wound her braid up atop her head and hid it under her cowboy hat, and with a small wave to her brother, she preceded Wally outside. "It's a beautiful night," she said. The stars were out, and there wasn't a cloud in the sky. It was cold enough they could see their breaths, but Frankie liked the cold. She always had.

He walked away from the road and toward the river that the ranch was named after. "How much of the property is yours?" he asked.

"Willard and I own all the land to the river. Beyond that is a quarter section that no one has claimed yet. I hope we can eventually expand out to there."

"There's just mountains there. What would anyone do with that?"

She shrugged. "I don't know, but those mountains are beautiful. They may not be practical, but imagine owning that majestic land."

As soon as they were a good distance from the road, he took her hand in his, marveling at how tiny it was. "I know I've said it before, but I can't believe anyone ever believed you were a man. Your hands are so tiny, and your fingers so slender."

She shrugged, blushing a bit. "I played the part well. And truly, I've not really left the ranch since we came here. Willard goes to town and talks about his brother, and everything assumes he's telling the truth. A few times men have come here for one reason or another, but they don't look beyond the obvious. Willard calls me his brother, so I must be his brother." She sighed. "Even when we've taken on ranch hands from time to time, and I cooked all the meals, no one ever thought anything of it."

"They were all blind. Even in your pants, you're the prettiest woman I've ever seen." The words felt foreign on his tongue. He wasn't used to complimenting young ladies, but he needed her to know how he felt.

Frankie felt the heat rising to her face. "Thank you." She'd been considered very pretty back home, but she felt like the wind had roughened her skin enough that she'd lost some of her beauty.

He led her to a fallen log and sat, pulling her down beside him. He still held her hand clutched in his. "Now that I've finally had a bath and don't smell so bad, what would you think about marrying me?"

She looked down at her feet for a moment, feeling overwhelmingly shy. She'd argued with the man at lunch, offered to wash his laundry, and fixed his meals. Now she was shy? "I think I'd like that."

He put his arm around her shoulders, wishing they weren't wearing coats. He couldn't even touch her this way. "May I kiss you?"

She nodded shyly, turning her head toward him and looking up at him. She was tiny and always had been, while he was huge. Even taller than Willard who was just about as tall as a church steeple. "I'd like that."

His free hand went to her cheek and cupped it tenderly. He lowered his lips to hers and touched them softly with his.

The tingling in the pit of her stomach increased, and she wrapped both arms around him, wishing there was less between them. His kiss was nice, and she suddenly wished it could go on forever.

When he pulled back, he was a bit out of breath. "How soon can we marry?"

"I'll have my dress done by Tuesday morning. We could go to town on Tuesday afternoon and tie the knot. You're willing to take Weston as your last name?"

He nodded. "I wouldn't have come here if I hadn't been. I'll happily give up Miller, because it just means that I was part of the demon horde."

She snuggled close to his side. "Good. Then let's make it happen on Tuesday. It will be my first time in town as a woman, but I doubt people will even realize I'm the same person. We can say Willard is my brother, and people won't realize I'm not another sibling."

"Is that what you want?"

She shrugged. "I'm really not sure. I thought I was brilliant pretending to be a man, but I never considered that the pretense would eventually have to end."

He sighed. "Well, either way, that's your decision. Just so people don't think you're a man after we're married. I'll give up my name for you, but I won't get that kind of reputation for you!"

"I won't ask you to. I'll probably still spend most of my time on the homestead."

"Does Willard do the shopping?"

She nodded. "He always has. It's just easier if I'm not seen."

"I see. And you want to keep it that way?"

"I guess I never really thought about it. I will though. I'll figure out exactly what I want to do before Tuesday. Does that work for you?" Her mind churned. She hated the idea of admitting to the whole town that she'd been lying about her gender for three years, but she wanted to be seen as a woman. She loved the idea of going into church on Wally's arm. "Do you care which way I go?"

"Yeah, I think I do. I'd rather everyone knew that you'd been pretending to be a man all along. I don't like the idea of deceptions. You're always found out. Trust me on this."

She nodded slowly. "I promise I'll take your feelings into account as I think about it."

"Thank you." He leaned down and kissed her once more, needing to convince himself that the first kiss hadn't been a fluke. There was something about this special woman that touched him in a way that no other woman had before. She was meant for him, just as he was meant for her. And their children were meant to be raised on this special ranch in Northern Idaho. River's End. It was just as beautiful as the visions the name had created in his mind.

She sighed contentedly. "We should get back to the house. Willard will come looking for us."

Wally shook his head. "No, I really don't think he will. He knew I wanted to ask you to marry me tonight."

"You didn't ask his permission, did you?" Though she knew that it was common for a man to ask a father or, in the father's absence, a brother for a woman's hand in marriage, she hated the idea in her case. She'd been on her own for too long, helping make the decisions that guided her own life. She was in charge of her destiny, and no man had the right to say if she could or could not marry.

He chuckled. "I didn't even think about it. I wouldn't have asked a lady to court me at home without her father's permission. Here I asked a woman to marry me, and it never once occurred to me that I should ask anyone. Is that strange?"

She shook her head. "I'm glad you didn't ask him. He and I are equal partners, and I'd have been angry if he'd said yes or no. It's my place to make those decisions for myself."

"Are you a suffragette?"

"I don't have a strong opinion on whether or not women should have the right to vote, but I do feel vehemently that women should be in charge of their own lives if they are old enough. And by old enough I mean seventeen or older!"

He nodded slowly. "All right. So if, as your husband, I tell you that you need to do something, how will you react?"

"It depends on what you tell me to do. If I think it's a good idea, I'll probably do it with minimal fuss. If you tell me to do something that's against my conscience or just plain stupid, then I won't. I have a brain, and I know how to use it."

Wally was surprised by her words, but he had to respect her for them. "All right. Thank you for telling me now, and not causing me to be shocked when we marry."

"Does that mean you're still marrying me?"

"Well, it's not like I didn't know that a woman who would ask her husband to change his name when they married wouldn't have odd ideas about who was in charge in a marriage."

"You think my ideas are odd?" she asked, pulling away from him to look at him by the light of the moon.

He shook his head adamantly. "That came out wrong. I don't think your ideas are odd so much as revolutionary. I like them though. I will do my best not to order you to do anything. We can decide together."

She sighed with relief. "Good. And just so you know if you ever tell me you're 'putting your foot down' over something, I might just have to burn your food for a week straight."

"Thank you for the warning. I will be sure never to use those particular words with you!" She shivered slightly, and he stood. "Let's get you back to the house and the warmth of the fire. I'm sorry I didn't realize you were cold. I was enjoying having some time alone with you."

"Don't apologize! I was enjoying it too."

He yawned, covering his mouth quickly with his hand. It must be past eight. He needed to get to bed, so he could wake before dawn again. He had to get more sleep. "I'm going to walk you to your door, and then go straight back to Willard's to go to sleep. I'm still tired from the train." His arm went around her shoulders and they walked back toward the house.

"Do you need to sleep late tomorrow? I'm sure Willard would understand."

He thought about it briefly before shaking his head. He wasn't going to do that and make a bad impression. There was nothing wrong with him. He was just tired. "No, I'll be fine."

"Are you sure? I can talk to Willard."

"Absolutely not. I might take a nap tomorrow afternoon, though. After we have our service. What time is that anyway?"

"We usually do our prayer reading right after breakfast. So around six. Do you want to start going into town to church after we marry?" She liked the idea even as she dreaded it.

"I've always gone to church on Sunday mornings, so it will seem odd to me if I don't. I would like to start going next week if you wouldn't mind too much."

"We always went back East too. It's just me pretending to be a man that has prevented us from being more a part of the community. It wouldn't surprise me if Willard found himself a girl at church soon if we start going. He was something of a charmer back home."

"Do you miss New York?" He'd thought she was perfectly content with her life in Idaho, but the last few minutes had been full of references to home.

"Sometimes. I mean life was easier there. I wasn't expected to do more than show up at balls in pretty gowns. Out here I don't know from one day to the next whether I'll be mending fences, chopping down trees, or helping a cow give birth. It's different. I love my life here, but back home it was simple. I was expected to choose a boy to marry and have babies. There was nothing else that I needed to worry about."

"What about babies?" he asked, studying her face by moonlight. "Do you want babies?"

She nodded. "I think I'd like to have at least a dozen."

He groaned. "Just promise me we'll discipline them. We don't need another demon horde."

Frankie smiled. "I promise you if people call my children the demon horde it will be because they are rude, not because my children are."

They'd reached her door, and he leaned down to kiss her softly. "Dream of me, Francine."

She smiled. "Are you always going to call me Francine?"

He nodded. "I can't think of you as Frankie."

"Good. I miss being Francine." She watched him as he walked toward Willard's cabin, smiling slightly. She was going to marry him, and he smelled good now.

Chapter Five

By Tuesday, Frankie was nervous. A lot more nervous than she'd thought she'd be. She'd had little time alone with Wally, and she was expected to share her bed with him that night? Really?

After lunch, he went back to Willard's cabin to get his things together and change into his wedding clothes, while she did the dishes and changed into her new dress. She wore her hair wound in a crown atop her head, a style she'd loved in her debutante days, but it felt strange now. She carefully smoothed the sides of her dress and stared in the mirror.

As a young lady, she'd spent a great deal of time sitting at a vanity table brushing her hair and imagining what her life would be like when she was married and a matron of society. She'd known who she'd marry from a very young age and she had always done her best to look perfect for him.

Then the rumors had started that Reginald, the man of her dreams, had married Katherine Elliott, her worst enemy, and that Katherine was already expecting a baby. Just about the same time, her only brother had been planning to move to Idaho and get some free land. She'd begged him to take her. Finally, after a month of begging, he'd agreed. She couldn't take the ignominy of being tossed aside for someone she hated.

That day she'd stopped spending time primping and started to work. She realized that she'd been little more than an empty-headed china doll back then, but now—she was a woman. She was strong and able to do the work of a man, while keeping house and doing the work of a woman. She knew there was nothing she was incapable of.

Which was why she'd decided to admit to her charade. When she and Wally stood before the pastor in Riston later, she would admit to her deception and tell him that she was the "brother" who had come

West with Willard. She dreaded it, but she knew it was the right thing to do. Besides, with Wally at her side, she could face them all.

She walked into the main room of her little house and opened the door, wondering what was keeping the men. The first thing she saw was Wally, standing there watching her. As soon as he saw her, he removed his hat and held it to his chest. "You look more beautiful than even I dreamed you would, Miss Francine."

She blushed prettily. "Thank you, Wally." She felt pretty too. For the first time in ages she felt absolutely beautiful. For whatever reason, putting on a dress made her feel like she'd been transformed into a lady again. A lady with the memory of how to muck out stalls and mend fences, sure, but a lady nonetheless.

He set his carpet bag just inside the door, before offering his hand to help her down the stairs in front of the house. "Willard has the wagon ready to drive us to town."

She pulled her shawl over her shoulders as she walked, thinking she should wear a hat, but she didn't care. It was the first time her hair had seen the light of day in three years, and she wasn't going to cover it. It was time for her to be a lady, and she was going to flaunt it.

Willard smiled at her, nodding slightly. From him it was high praise.

Wally helped her into the wagon and got up beside her, covering their laps with a blanket. "That dress is beautiful. I had no idea you knew how to sew."

A smile touched her lips. "Willard and I were raised in an affluent household, but our mama believed girls should know how to keep a house. We were taught to cook, sew, clean, knit, crochet...well if you can name something a frontier wife should do, we were taught it. I can also waltz perfectly, play piano, and carry a tune."

Wally shook his head at her. "How did I end up with such a prize?"

She swallowed hard. "When I sent that letter to your sister, I told Willard that if anyone was willing to agree to all my terms, it would be a mail order miracle. That's what you are to me. My miracle."

He smiled. "I like that. I've never been anyone's miracle before. I was usually the one being chased off someone's property because no one trusted me with their daughters...or livestock for that matter."

"Why would they fear for their livestock?" Willard asked.

"Well, there was one incident where my siblings and I decided to paint the cow. We took our Pa's newspaper and spread it out on the barn floor and we made Mabel, the cow, stand on it. For some reason, we saw nothing wrong with painting the cow, but we were worried about what would happen if we got paint on the barn floor." Wally shook his head. "The story got around town way too fast for my tastes."

Willard blinked a couple of times. "I hope your children don't act like you do."

Frankie rolled her eyes. "I can assure you, they won't. My children will be raised with manners, and nowhere in the world is it mannerly to paint a cow."

"Or throw apples with worms in them at wagons driving by from the top of the apple tree?" Wally asked.

She just shook her head. "How long has it been since you stopped considering yourself a member of this demon horde?"

Wally thought about it for a moment. He'd probably stopped acting the fool with his siblings when Elizabeth had moved out, so it had been a while. "Seven years I think? When my sister moved out to take over the mail order bride business, I became one of the oldest left at home, and more responsibilities landed on me. It became more important to help make a living than tie the teacher into the outhouse during lunchtime."

Willard snickered. "We talked about doing that a couple of times. You really did it?"

Wally shrugged. "It seemed like the thing to do at the time."

"Did you ever put snakes in the teacher's desk?"

"Oh yeah. With every new teacher. And we never had a teacher last more than a semester, because of our shenanigans. It was always my brothers and sisters and I pulling the pranks, but the whole class loved the extra recesses they got out of it. Of course none of them were stuck with the name 'demon horde' following them around for the rest of their lives."

Frankie smiled at him. "I'm glad you learned to be responsible and came to Idaho. Now I won't worry how people will think about me for pretending to be a man, because I know if we go back to your home town, people will think even worse of you."

"Well, that's not exactly fair!" Wally responded, but then he shrugged. "I guess it doesn't really matter though. How often are we going to go all the way back to Beckham?"

Frankie shrugged. "I don't know. It might be interesting to hear what the people there have to say about you." They stopped in front of the church, and she allowed Wally to help her down. As she walked past him, she whispered, "Exactly what color did you and your siblings decide was right to paint a cow?"

"Oh, lavender of course. You never paint a cow any other hue but lavender. I mean, really, was there any question?"

Frankie was laughing as she walked past him into the church. They found the preacher at the front, practicing his sermon. "Reverend Maddix?"

The preacher looked out at them. "What can I help you with?"

Frankie walked straight to the preacher, took a deep breath, and said, "I'm not sure if you remember me. I'm Frankie Weston."

The preacher scrunched up his face, obviously thinking. "Of course I remember Frankie Weston...but...Frankie's a man."

"I was just pretending to be a man so I could run around in pants and do a man's work. I'm here to get married. This is my fiancé, Wallace Miller."

The old man looked back and forth between Frankie and Wally. "Are you sure you want to marry her? She's been pretending to be a man for an awful long time."

Wally smiled at Frankie, taking her hand in his. "I'm sure. I knew she was pretending to be a man from the moment I met her." He didn't mention being a mail order groom, which pleased Frankie. It was bad enough that she would always have the stigma of pretending to be a man, but she didn't want it to be known she'd sent away for a husband.

"Would you mind marrying us, Reverend Maddix?"

The reverend shook his head, looking over at Willard. "You give your permission for this marriage?"

Willard crossed his arms and shook his head. "I don't need to. Frankie has been my equal partner since we decided to journey West. She's a lot more capable of choosing a man who will make her happy than I am."

The reverend frowned. "Are you going to give her away?"

He shook his head. "There's no need. As I said, it's Frankie's choice."

Frankie looked at her brother for a moment before tearing herself away from Wally. She threw herself at Willard, doing her best not to blubber as she hugged him tightly. "You're the best big brother a girl ever had."

Willard smiled. "And you're the best little sister, pretending to be a brother. Now go get married."

He stood behind Wally and Frankie as they said their vows. When the reverend told Wally to kiss his bride, she stepped closer, raising her lips to his. The kiss was so much more than a kiss to her. It was a promise for the future. It was the hope of a family being raised on Weston land. It was the miracle Frankie had needed.

"I wish you much happiness, Mr. Miller," Reverend Maddix said, once Wally had raised his head.

"Oh, I'm taking her name," Wally said with a grin. "Call me 'Mr. Weston.'" The three Westons were laughing at the baffled look on the officiant's face as they left the church. "See you on Sunday!"

When they reached the wagon, Wally held out his hand to help her up. Just as she was gathering her skirts to climb, someone stopped and stared at her. "Francine Weston? Is that you?"

Frankie looked over at the sound of the familiar voice, and her heart sank. "Reginald. What are you doing in Idaho?"

"Looking for you."

"Why? You're a married man, and I'm a married woman." She looked at Wally with a smile, not wanting him to think she'd forgotten him.

"When did you marry?" Reginald asked, obviously surprised.

"About ten minutes ago. Wally, this is Reginald White. We knew each other back home. Reginald, this is my husband Wallace." She didn't give the last name Weston, because she was sure Reginald would make fun of him for taking her last name, and she wouldn't subject her new husband to ridicule.

The two men looked at each other, and Willard came around the wagon. "Reginald, you have no business being here. Go home to your wife and child." He stepped between Frankie and Reginald, making it clear the other man had no right to his sister.

"They're dead. They both died of the measles. I never loved Katherine anyway, so I came here to find Francine. I guess I'm too late." Reginald shook his head. "That's what you got married in? I'd have thought a lady like Francine would wear something that was more...appropriate to her station in life."

Wally nodded. "You're very much too late. Goodbye, Reginald." He took Frankie's hand to help her into the wagon, and she accepted it, moving as if in a daze.

Once he'd climbed in beside her, Wally stared straight ahead as Willard began the drive back to the ranch. They were halfway home before anyone spoke. "Who was that man, Francine? Did you love him?"

Frankie sighed heavily. "I don't know. I don't think so. He was my escort for my debutante ball back in another lifetime. We had talked about marriage, and I was expecting a proposal any day. Then one day, he just stopped coming around. I couldn't figure out what was wrong until I heard that he'd married my arch-enemy Katherine. She was expecting his baby, so the marriage was forced, but that was the end of that. I asked Willard if I could come West with him that day."

Wally frowned. "And how did you feel seeing him today? Are those feelings still there?"

She shook her head immediately. "No, not at all. I felt more shock than anything else. I just wanted him to leave, so we could go home. I would choose you over him any day."

Wally said nothing more as he watched the scenery go by. He hated that the man had come on his wedding day of all days. He hoped she remembered who she was married to.

"I'm starving. What's for supper, Frankie?" Willard asked, obviously trying to ease the tension.

"I put a pot roast in before we left. Wally said it was one of his favorite meals, so I thought he should have it on his wedding day." She reached out and wound her fingers through Wally's hoping he'd understand the gesture was one of apology.

Wally sighed. Her brother was going to be there for their wedding supper. Why hadn't he thought of that before? Their situation was odd. Very odd. Maybe he just needed to get used to being part of a family of three, instead of a couple. He should have known from the letter, shouldn't he? She'd mentioned a brother in it. Who mentioned their brother when they were sending away for a groom? For that matter, who sends away for a groom? The whole situation was odd.

Frankie felt horrible. She hadn't asked Reginald to come, but he'd been there anyway. Now what was she supposed to do? It was her wedding night, and her groom was obviously upset with her.

Why couldn't life be simple?

Chapter Six

After supper, a meal where little was spoken, and Willard disappeared as quickly as he could, Frankie put on a large apron and did the supper dishes. Wally was saying little to her, and she didn't know how to get his mind off Reginald.

When the dishes were done, she walked to him and sat down, taking his hand in hers. "I'm very sorry you found out about Reginald that way. I didn't think he'd ever show up around here. I didn't even know he knew where I was."

"He's definitely not the kind of man I can see a woman who knows how to mend fences marry."

Frankie laughed. "Oh never. He was always the escort of the prettiest girl in town. He was my beau for a year, but I don't think I ever really knew him. I thought I loved him, because he was what my parents wanted for me, but he wasn't really what I wanted if that makes sense."

"It makes a lot of sense to me. I guess I never really thought of you as a woman who was above me socially. And now I have to."

"Why do you have to? I'm the woman you came here to marry. I do all the chores on my own. I don't have a maid or a cook or anyone else helping me. I'm the woman you see in front of you. There *is* no social class out here. There're only mountains, trees, rivers, and cattle. Together, we will turn this ranch into something that people will envy for miles around."

"So you don't regret marrying me?"

She smiled. "No, I don't regret marrying you. I mean I'm nervous, because I've married a man I've only known for a few days, but even if you hadn't been here, I'd never have married Reginald. He's not the right man for me. He'd never put up with my wearing britches."

Wally frowned. He didn't want to put up with her wearing britches either! "You'll wear dresses now that we're married, right?"

She shrugged. "This is the only dress I have, so probably not all the time. I need to get more fabric to make a couple more of them. And then there will always be occasions where I'm needed to do some work on the ranch. I'll have to wear pants for some things. I know you prefer me in a dress, but it won't always be feasible."

"But you'll wear one as much as you can?"

She nodded. "I should make a trip into town tomorrow then. If I'd known you felt so strongly about it, I'd have bought fabric for another dress today. I thought you didn't mind my britches."

He shrugged. "I don't mind them, because I recognize their necessity in the past. But not so much in the future. Yes, you'll need to wear them from time to time, but I'd rather my wife didn't run around town looking like a man."

"Then I won't." It would be a hard promise to keep, but she'd do her very best. "I'll only wear them on days when I absolutely need to. And I'll get enough fabric for two every-day dresses tomorrow."

"Can we afford that?"

She nodded. "We're doing fine financially. We had some money when we came here, and the ranch is already paying for itself. I can afford to buy fabric for a couple of new dresses." She didn't tell him exactly how much money, because she knew it would shock him. She and her brother had been given money by their father to leave, and it had been a generous amount. He'd been proud they'd been willing to strike out on their own.

"Then it's a good plan." He got to his feet. "Why don't you get ready for bed, while I go for a quick walk?" He was eager to get on with the wedding night. He'd waited his whole life for this.

Frankie swallowed hard. This was the part of the night she was unsure about. How could she submit to a man she barely knew? "All right."

Wally leaned over and kissed her softly, needing to remind himself that she was still his. Reginald hadn't changed anything.

She watched him leave, and then she rushed into her bedroom, changing into her nightgown and taking her hair down. She ran her brush through it quickly, having long forgotten the one hundred strokes she was supposed to give it every night according to her mother. She put it into a long braid, her fingers flying. She had no idea how much time he'd give her, and she wanted to be ensconced under the covers before he came back in.

She slipped between the sheets, her arms at her side, and closed her eyes, taking deep breaths. Why this was so frightening to her, she didn't know. Her mother had never talked to her about it, but she'd had some friends who had married before she did, and they'd explained everything to her. They'd even talked as if they enjoyed it, so her fear was irrational.

When Wally came into the room, he turned down the lantern and undressed in the dark. More than anything he wanted to see his bride, but by the way she was covered, he could tell she was nervous. So was he for that matter. What if he couldn't do it right? What if she didn't enjoy it? He wanted her to like it, because then she'd want to do it more. He knew he'd like it. There was no doubt about that.

He slid into the bed beside her, reaching for her, but she didn't turn to him and instead stayed where she was with her arms straight at her sides. "You're going to have to cooperate for this to happen," he told her softly.

"I don't know what to do!" She could hear the panic in her voice as she said it, and she was ashamed. Every woman in the world went through this on their wedding night, so why did she feel like she was so different?

Wally sighed, his hand stroking the arm closest to him. "I don't either, really. We'll have to figure it out together."

She turned on her side facing him, trying to make out his features in the dark. "You mean you've never done it either?"

"No, I haven't. Remember, no one would let me court their daughters. Besides, I was taught that making love was only allowed after marriage with your wife. I wouldn't have done it with anyone else."

She reached out and stroked his cheek. "And you don't think I'm crazy for being afraid?"

"Not at all. I'm pretty nervous. I mean I understand the mechanics of it all, but what if I do it wrong? What if I don't please you?"

She blinked in surprise a couple of times. "You care about pleasing me?" She'd been told that not all men did. She wished she could forget everything she knew about how this night was supposed to go and just let herself feel.

"Of course I do! I want you to want to do this as much as I will. And I have a feeling I'm going to want to do it a lot."

She giggled. "Well, I've heard that's true of all men."

"You have?" he asked, his voice full of mock-anger. "And just who have you been talking to about this?"

She shrugged. "Just some friends from back home."

"Do you have any female friends here?" he asked softly.

She shook her head. "No, because I've had to stay in disguise for so long. I'm hoping that when we start going to church every Sunday I'll be able to make some. I can't wait to make friends, really."

"I think that'll be good for you." He couldn't help but wonder if there was a doctor in town who could help her when it was time to have babies, or if they'd be on their own. Riston seemed like a tiny town with a church, a store, and little else. He gathered her close, having her rest her head on his shoulder. Maybe if they talked for a while, she'd calm down a little.

"Tell me what you see for the future of the ranch," he said, stroking one arm as he snuggled her close.

She sighed. "I see more the potential of family on the ranch. I want to have a dozen kids and all of them stay right here, working to build up our home. We could turn it into a community right here. Wouldn't it be nice if we had several ranch hands, a blacksmith, and even a little general store right here on the ranch? I can almost picture it. And a chapel. Our very own chapel."

"Would all that make you happy?"

"I don't need all that to make me happy, Wally. I'm happy just lying here with you, talking in the dark about the future. I believe that happiness comes from within. The whole thing with Reginald destroyed my ability to believe in myself for a long time. I thought that it meant that I wasn't good enough to marry. But really, it just meant that he didn't have it in *him* to control his lust. It had nothing to do with me at all. Never again will I let my happiness be wrapped up in things around me. It has to come from me."

"And how do you make that happen?" he asked, surprised at her words. He had always looked at happiness as almost something that you absolutely couldn't control. It was something that happened because you met a goal, or because of the person who was by your side, not because it was something you just were.

"It's a choice I make every day. I can wake up and think about how hard life is, or I can embrace it and be happy anyway. I wake up and I know I have to mend fences, which is my least favorite ranch chore, and I choose to be happy, because it's not something I have to do every day. Because I'm good at it, and I can get it done quickly. Because I have the full use of both of my hands and legs, and I know how to work hard. I'd rather stay in the house and bake bread all day. I love to bake bread. I love the smell of it as it's coming out of the oven. So if I have to mend fences, I can think about how much I'm really going to enjoy the next day I get to stay in the house and bake bread all day. I choose to find happiness in everything I do, instead of choosing to be sad or angry."

"And how did you find happiness when you saw Reginald today?"

She giggled. "I found happiness when I saw him, because I knew that I'm not married to him. I dodged that bullet, and I'm married to a truly good man, running a ranch that I love. I'm not back in New York trying to live up to society's expectations."

He smiled. "Very good answer. Your new husband approves."

"And I approve of my new husband!" She kissed his bare shoulder softly. "How did your sister come to run a mail order bride agency? Is she married?"

He shook his head. "No, she's not, but I think she's going to realize sooner or later what's right under her nose. Her butler, Bernard, is the perfect man for her, and I hope someday she marries him."

"But how did she get there?"

"Well, our oldest sister, Susan, became a mail order bride around 1883, I think. She moved to Fort Worth and married a rancher there. Then a couple of years later, Elizabeth, the second oldest, went into town and she ran into the matchmaker. They'd lost contact, but Elizabeth had always liked her and respected the work she did. The matchmaker was off to become a mail order bride herself, so she asked Elizabeth to take it over. She provided her with a house, found her a butler, and everything. So Harriett moved to Seattle, and Elizabeth moved into one of the biggest homes in Beckham. It was all very strange."

"It sounds like it." She lightly traced a pattern on his shoulder. "Are you talking to me to make me less nervous? Or have you decided we should wait before we...you know?"

He smiled. "I thought talking might calm you down a bit. Were you hoping I'd decided to wait?"

She shook her head. "No, but I'm feeling much calmer, and I think if we're going to try to do this thing, we should maybe get going with it. I need to get up early to make breakfast and feed you two hungry men."

He sighed at that. "Is Willard going to eat every meal with us forever?"

"Until he finds a wife he will. He's my brother, and I'm not going to let him eat his own cooking. I got sick once, and he cooked for me for a week. I've never eaten so many disgusting concoctions in my entire life."

"All right." He dropped a kiss on her nose, and she immediately shifted until their lips met.

"You missed," she whispered against his lips, her hands stroking his bare shoulders.

He laughed. "I didn't miss at all. I just thought it would be easier to ease you into it."

"No need to ease me into anything." She took his hand and placed it on her breast. "I think it's time to get this show on the road."

"You, my sweet wife, are awfully demanding. I guess I should have known who'd wear the pants in this family."

"Well for now, it's both of us, but I don't think that makes it so I'm in charge. We'll be in charge together. Making decisions together is the way to have a good marriage in my opinion."

"Well, I think we'll have a better marriage if you just close your eyes and enjoy yourself for a few minutes. No decisions need to be made. We just need to feel."

She wrapped her arms around his neck and pressed herself closer to him. "Is that so?"

"It is so!"

She wriggled closer but said nothing else for a long while.

Afterward, she lay with her head on his shoulder again, her hand toying with the light covering of hair on his chest. "That wasn't nearly as bad as I thought it would be."

"A ringing endorsement from my new wife. Tomorrow night we'll shoot for, 'Not half bad.' By the time we've been married for a week, I expect to hear, 'That was wonderful. Can we do it again?' Is that understood?"

She laughed. "You earn it, and I'll say it!"

He pressed a kiss to the top of her head. "Sleep, my wife. We need to work tomorrow." He lay beside her thinking about the pleasure she'd brought him. He definitely needed to get better at it, because he was going to want that a lot.

Chapter Seven

When Frankie woke the following morning, she hurried from bed and dressed quickly, hoping she could be in the kitchen fully clothed and cooking before Wally woke up. As she tiptoed from the room, she saw that he was still on his side as she'd left him, and she went to the kitchen to put a pot of coffee on.

Willard came in while she was cooking breakfast, giving her an assessing look. "You all right?" he asked gruffly. It was obvious by his face he'd worried about her.

She nodded, blushing slightly. "I'm fine. Breakfast will be ready in a few minutes."

"Wally still sleeping?"

"Yes. I don't think he's had enough sleep since he got here, so I let him steal a few more minutes, before he absolutely *had* to be up."

Willard poured himself a cup of coffee and sat down at the table. "What are your plans for today?"

"I was hoping you'd take me into town. It's important to Wally that I wear a dress whenever possible, so I'm going to make a couple more, but I need fabric."

"And you don't trust your favorite brother to pick out the fabric for your dresses?" He nodded to her dress. "I wondered why you were looking so fancy today."

"No, you *know* I don't trust you. Well? Will you take me into town?"

He nodded. "Or I can stay here and work, and we can let your new husband drive you."

Her heart leapt at the idea. She wanted more time alone with her new husband. "I'd like that if you don't mind."

He shook his head. "Not at all. And if there's something left from dinner last night, I'll have that for my lunch and you two can eat in town."

Frankie nodded eagerly. There was a small diner in town where she'd never dared to eat. Willard said her delicate way of wiping her mouth would give her away immediately. "Thank you!"

"It's no problem. Now that you're married, maybe it's time for us to take on a ranch hand permanently. It will help to have Wally here, of course, but we could grow so much faster with one more man."

She tilted her head to one side, considering. One of the reasons no one had ever stayed on long was because she was afraid her secret would be found. Now that she was married and had no secret, it wouldn't be so hard on her for someone to stay on the ranch. "Let's do it. Do you want me to put feelers out in town today?"

"I'll write up a note for you to pin on the bulletin board in the mercantile."

"I'd appreciate it." She served him a plate of bacon with scrambled eggs. Looking toward the bedroom, she frowned. "I should go wake Wally."

"Nah. Let him sleep. You two take today as a honeymoon. I'm sorry you can't take more. And you'll still have to cook supper, because I'm not willing to starve."

"So really our honeymoon consists of lunch in town and him taking the day off."

Willard shrugged. "You missed being a girl. Women never really get a day off. You knew that."

She sighed. "I did." She carried her own plate to the table, sitting down to eat with her brother. "Are you sure we should let him sleep?"

"He's been yawning since the moment he got here. Let the man sleep. Store in town doesn't open until nine anyway. You can get him up at eight and get there by then. But if you're wanting to time it with lunch, wake him at ten thirty. Then you can get the shopping done before you eat."

She nodded, forking up a bite of her breakfast. "Is there anything else you need me to do for you while we're in town? Any errands? Anything you need from the store?"

"I'm needing some socks. The ones I'm wearing have been darned so often, they're giving me blisters. Maybe you could get the yarn to make me a couple more pair?"

"Sure. What color do you want?"

He raised an eyebrow at her. "Why do you think I'd care at all? My sock will be hidden in my boot. What difference does it make?"

"Lavender it is!"

"To match Wally's family cow?"

Frankie giggled and shook her head. "Those kids were rotten! I refuse to spoil a child the way they all must have been spoiled."

"I'm glad to hear it. I don't want to go into church one Sunday morning and hear about how awful my nephews and nieces are. I'll be mending fences just this side of the river today. If you'll leave my lunch in the oven, I'll pull it out when I'm ready to eat."

They'd made it a habit since they'd moved to Idaho that if he was working on his own for a day, he always told her where he'd be. They never knew if something would happen, and she'd need to search for him. "Thank you. I'll have supper ready at five."

"You always do."

She'd always stopped working a couple of hours early, so she could have supper ready, and she'd made certain to have enough for lunch the next day. It had only taken a couple of months of trial and error to hit on the perfect schedule for them. "I'm going to write to Mother and Father and let them know I got married."

"Make sure to make mention of the fact that you got married in a dress. That will make Mother happier than anything else possibly could."

Frankie laughed. “She will be ecstatic.” Their proper mother had never been able to wrap her mind around the fact that her eldest daughter ran around mending fences while wearing men’s britches.

It was after ten when Wally wandered out of the bedroom, rubbing his eyes. “Why did you let me sleep so late? I should be helping Willard!” He was fully dressed and already heading for the door.

“Willard said we should take today as a honeymoon...at least until it’s time for me to cook his supper. He suggested we have lunch at the diner in town and pick up some fabric for more dresses for me. And he wants some socks.” She held up the note her brother had written. “I’m also going to hang this on the bulletin board in the store. He wants to hire on one more man now that I’m married.”

“Now that you’re married?” Wally looked confused. “I thought you’d had hired men before.”

“We did, but we were never willing to keep one on for long, because we were worried my secret would be out. Now that I’m married, that’s no longer a worry. We’ll grow a lot faster if we have one more man doing the work. And then I can be inside full time, which is my goal anyway.”

He walked to her, dropping a soft kiss on her lips. “Good morning, Francine.”

She smiled. “Good morning, Wally. I’ll get you a cup of coffee, and I can get you something to eat if you’d like, but we’ll be eating in a couple of hours in town anyway.” She carried a cup of coffee to him and sat down for the first time in a couple of hours. Despite having agreed to take the day mostly off, she had scrubbed the kitchen floor and cleaned the windows. She hated to be idle, which is something she’d never thought would happen. “Do you need anything from the store while we’re in town?”

He shrugged. “I could probably use a pair of gloves and a scarf. I forgot mine back home.” Truthfully he’d left them so his younger siblings could use them. There was always a shortage of cold weather clothes at the Miller farm.

"We can do that. How are your socks? I'm making a couple pair for Willard."

"I could use socks too." He frowned. "I only have a couple pairs of pants, two shirts, a suit, and a coat. And my boots of course."

"So any sewing or knitting I want to do for you would be appreciated?"

He nodded. "I would say that."

"All right. We'll pick out what we need in town today." She saw he'd finished his cup of coffee. "Whenever you're ready we can head out."

"Sounds good." He took her hand and brought it to his lips. "I'm glad you married me."

She smiled sweetly. "I am too. I'm a little nervous about going to town though."

"Are you afraid to run into Reginald again?"

"No, that's not it at all. If I run into him, it won't be a big deal. He was in my past, but he's no longer in my life."

"Why are you nervous then?" he asked, not understanding.

"Because I've been deceiving the good people of Riston for three years now. I'm afraid they'll remember that and hate me." Frankie looked down at her hands nervously, fidgeting in her chair. "I really don't know what to expect, but I don't expect anyone to come up to me and tell me what a great joke it was that I played on them all."

"I guess not. Well, either way, you'll have my full support."

Once they were on their way to town, she was surprised how good it felt to be sitting beside her handsome husband, wearing a dress. Yes, the pants she'd grown used to were a great deal more comfortable, but the dress made her feel feminine for a change. When they reached the mercantile in town, Wally parked the wagon and reached up for her, grabbing her waist and lifting her down.

She smiled up at him. "I think you're just supposed to take my hand to help me down," she said softly.

"I like doing things my way. I get to touch you more."

"I like it too." Her voice was soft, and she looked around her hoping no one had overheard.

He offered his arm, and she took it, walking into the store with him. She immediately walked back to the yard goods and looked through several different prints of calico.

"Francine! I'm surprised to see you in town two days in a row. And in the same dress. Have you fallen into poverty?" Reginald asked from behind her.

"Of course not." She turned away from the man she now considered odious and went back to choosing the fabric. "Which do you like, Wally?" Her voice was soft and sweet.

Wally frowned at the two different fabrics. "I like the mint green. It matches your eyes. And I think I like the lavender. Then you'll match how Mabel looked on that special day."

Reginald looked back and forth between the newlyweds. "Have you been married before as well, Wally?"

"No, I haven't." Wally refused to say anything else. The man seemed to be following them.

After Frankie chose the two fabrics she wanted for dresses, they moved on to the yarn. She chose a very bright shade of red and an equally vibrant shade of blue for her brother's socks. "Go ahead and choose four of five colors for socks. I'll choose for your scarf and gloves."

"Are you actually going to sew and knit yourself?" Reginald asked, his voice full of surprise.

"My mother taught me to sew and knit from a very young age. I can also cook. Mother said if our husbands ever fell on hard times, we'd be able to feed and clothe our families anyway."

She and Wally wandered to the dry goods, and she chose some flour and sugar. "We didn't have a wedding cake last night, so I thought I could make a cake tomorrow. You do like sweets, don't you?"

"Love them," Wally replied. "I just wish there was a dessert as sweet as my wife."

She laughed softly, her eyes meeting his. She knew she was pretending to some extent, because she had a need for Reginald to believe she was very much in love with her husband. After they'd chosen everything they needed, she gave the note her brother had written to Mr. Larson, the owner of the mercantile. "My brother and I have a need for a hired hand. Would you mind posting that on your bulletin board?"

"Not at all, Miss...?"

"You know me. I'm Frankie Weston," she said softly, hoping Reginald wouldn't hear.

"Wait...Frankie? You're a man!"

She smiled tightly at Mr. Larson, knowing his voice had carried throughout the store. "I felt the need to disguise myself, but now that I've married, I'm happy to be known as a woman again." She gestured to the wagon outside the front door. "If you'd be kind enough to load our purchases, my husband and I will be on our way to the diner. I haven't eaten another woman's cooking in a very long time, and I'd like to rectify that." Without looking behind her to see if Reginald had heard her, she walked toward the door, her hand on Wally's arm.

As soon as they were outside, Wally looked down at her. "He's getting to you."

"He's making me angry. He has no right to come out here and follow me around everywhere. I've moved on with my life, and it's time he realized it." She stopped in front of the diner, and waited while Wally opened the door for her.

It wasn't long before they were seated and had ordered their lunch. Reginald came in and sat at the table beside them, watching them as he sipped at a cup of coffee but ordering nothing.

Once they'd eaten, Frankie reached out and grasped Wally's hand, giving him the money she had intended to pay for the meal with. She didn't want Wally to be embarrassed of his wife paying, but more importantly, she didn't want Reginald to see her pay. She didn't need him to draw any conclusions about who wore the pants in her family...especially now that he heard she'd been running around disguised as a man.

She felt her old beau's eyes on her as she left the diner, still clinging to Wally's arm. "Take me home. I can't wait to spend the afternoon, just the two of us."

Wally watched her but said nothing. He knew she was uncomfortable around her old beau, but he didn't like the way she felt the need to pretend there was more between them than there was. What was Reginald still doing in town anyway? He should have been on a train to New York by now. He'd have to talk to Willard about the situation. Maybe his brother-in-law would have some answers.

Chapter Eight

Frankie and Wally went for a long walk that afternoon, and she showed him all her favorite places on the ranch. They stopped at the huge pine tree in the front yard first. It was over seven feet tall. "I love this tree. Every year Willard asks me if I want him to cut it down and bring it into the house, because he knows I consider it the perfect Christmas tree, and every year I tell him we need to leave it in the yard, so it can continue to grow and our children can enjoy it as well. I string popcorn for it, and the birds all eat it." As she said it, she thought that it might be nice if she made him a special ornament for the tree that year, and she decided that she would do just that.

As they walked, she talked about what it was like when they first arrived in the summer of 1889. They'd lived in a small tent as they'd worked all day every day to build first her house and then one for him. As soon as she'd had a kitchen to cook in, and a room to sleep in, they'd started on his cabin. The stable had been the third building to be built, and then the small barn.

The cattle hadn't really come until the spring of 1890, because they had taken the whole winter to clear as many trees from their main area as they could. She was proud of the work they'd done on the ranch, and proud that her hands had helped to do it.

"You seem to be very happy here," he said.

She nodded emphatically. "I am. I'm ready for children though."

"I guess that's where I come in," he said, winking at her and making her blush.

"I think that would be the case." She rested her head against his shoulder for a moment as they walked on further down by the river. She knew that's where Willard was working, so she deliberately walked as far from the area her brother would be in as possible. She just had to be close to the river with her new husband, because it was the most romantic spot on the ranch. It just wasn't possible to take a romantic walk when she was constantly running into her elder brother.

"And I know I'm also here to help with the chores."

"And for me. I needed the companionship."

He looked at her with surprise. "You did?"

"Of course I did. This marriage wasn't self-sacrificing. I was ready to not be alone all winter long. I'd hoped we'd marry by Christmas, and we beat Christmas by six weeks."

He smiled. "What does my beautiful bride want for Christmas?"

She shrugged, blushing a little. "I don't know."

"Yes, you do. I can see it on your face."

"Well, I'd love to know we were expecting our first baby by Christmas time. Don't you think that would be a perfect gift for both of us?"

"I would like that as well. Maybe we should have gotten you some extra yarn so you could knit little booties."

She grinned. "You know I thought about that, but I'd be afraid that starting on them would make it harder for us to conceive."

"I'm willing to do what it takes to have a baby on the way by Christmas. You can count on me."

Frankie laughed, blushing. "You need to stop teasing me, Wallace Weston!"

"Wallace Weston. You know, I'm surprised at how much I like the sound of that. I do have a question, though."

"What's that?"

"In your letter you said you wanted a man who was willing to take the Weston last name, and I had no problem understanding that. What I don't understand is that you wanted a man with a given name that started with W. Why was that?"

"It's a tradition in my family that all men have names starting with W. Willard, Wellesley, Walton, Walter, Ward...you get the idea. So I wanted to have a man whose first name started with a W, so he'd do well with the other Weston men. I'm glad you didn't have to change your first name."

"I think that's why my sister thought of me first when she read your letter."

Frankie stopped walking, looking up at him. "I'm glad she thought of you. I'm starting to have feelings for you, Wally."

He smiled down at her. "I have a whole lot of feelings for you already."

It wasn't his words so much as the way he said them that made her blush. She loved being a newlywed.

*****

Two weeks later, Frankie was in the kitchen wearing one of the new dresses she'd made and just about to drop dumplings into a pot of chicken and broth. She had never made chicken and dumplings, but she'd gotten the recipe from a new friend at church, and she was eager to try it.

There was a pounding at the door, and she grabbed the revolver that always stayed with her while the men were out on the ranch. Tucking it into the pocket of her apron, she went to the door, opening it cautiously.

Reginald stood in front of her. "I thought I'd find you home."

"Is there something you need?" She wanted to ask why he was still in Idaho, but she knew that would be too rude. Her mother would be disgusted with her for as rude as she'd already been.

"I just want to talk to you. May I come in?"

She shook her head, stepping outside, keeping her hand on the pistol in her pocket. "Tell me why you're here."

"I just want to apologize for how things ended between us. When I knew Katherine was pregnant, I should have come to you and told you myself instead of letting you hear it from someone else."

"Yes, you should have." She wasn't going to give him an inch. She wanted nothing to do with him ever again.

"I've always regretted how I treated you. I feel awful for it. Will you forgive me?"

Frankie sighed. "Truthfully, there's nothing to forgive. I've moved on. I'm married now—quite happily I may add. I don't care what happened all those years ago, and I certainly don't need you here reminding me of how stupid I was."

He frowned. "You weren't stupid. I figured someday I'd move West with you and we'd have a place like this together. Then I find out you have a ranch out here with your brother!"

"I couldn't stay in town with everyone whispering behind my back. You hurt me. I've grown up, and I'm over it. I'm happy now. I'd appreciate it if you went right back to New York where you came from."

Reginald eyed her shrewdly. "I will if you tell me how you met your husband. No one had ever heard of him until you married him, and he took your last name instead of the other way around. That doesn't happen. So how'd you end up married to him?"

"That's really none of your business, Reginald. I met him, we courted, and we married. That's all you really need to know." She still stood on the steps, and over his head she saw Wally and Willard approaching. She wasn't sure if she was thankful they were coming to get him away from her, or worried about Wally being upset that she was talking to him alone. She knew Wally didn't trust him even a little bit.

Her brother walked up on one side of him, and Wally went to the other. "Why are you here, White?" Willard asked, his voice deceptively soft. Frankie could hear the threat in it.

"I had to apologize for my bad behavior to Francine. I hoped I could talk her into running off with me, but she claims to be happily married."

Frankie hardened her jaw. "I'm going to go inside and finish making supper while you men take care of the refuse." She immediately went inside, slamming the door behind her. She didn't care what they did with him. She dropped the dumplings into the boiling broth and covered the pot. Now supper would be late thanks to Reginald. The man needed to get out of her life and stay out of it.

She was serving the chicken and dumplings into three bowls when the door opened behind her. She didn't bother to turn. "Francine, we need to talk about him." Wally's voice was quiet, but he was much too serious for her tastes.

She sighed heavily. "After supper. I refuse to air our dirty laundry in front of my brother." There was nothing to air, of course, but she worried that Wally wouldn't think that.

Five minutes later, Willard came into the house, taking a deep sniff of the air. "Something smells good. When did you learn to cook this, Frankie?"

She shrugged. "Wally mentioned one of his favorite meals was chicken and dumplings, so I asked Mary, my new friend at church. She wrote down the recipe for me, and I decided to try it tonight. I thought my new husband would appreciate it if I got a little more inventive in the kitchen."

Wally frowned at her. "Of course, I appreciate it! It smells wonderful."

Once they'd prayed, Wally took his first bite, sighing with contentment. "My sister Elizabeth was always the one with a knack for making chicken and dumplings in our house. I thought she was the best cook of all my sisters, but then she moved away. She invited me to supper after she got your letter, and I have to admit, I'd hoped she was making chicken and dumplings for me, but she didn't."

"That's too bad," Willard responded.

"These are ten times better than Elizabeth's ever were. Your dumplings are perfect, Francine. Thank you for making the effort to learn to cook something new for me."

She simply nodded. She wanted to say so much, but Willard was there, and she would wait until he was gone.

"I told him to go back to New York and not show his face here again," Willard suddenly put in, eating a bite of the chicken. "I'm going to write to Father as well. I'm certain his parents don't realize he's here causing trouble."

"Will they do something about it?" Wally asked. "What can they do? He's an adult."

"He's also their heir. They can threaten his inheritance, and nothing matters more to Reginald than money. I'm sure he'll go home after his father sends for him. He won't risk missing out on money."

"Is his family wealthy?" Wally asked, feeling stupid as soon as the words left his mouth. Of course he was stupid. Why would her wealthy parents have approved of him as an escort for their daughter otherwise?

Willard shrugged. "Not nearly as wealthy as our family, but they do pretty well for themselves."

As soon as she was finished eating, Frankie carried the rest of the pot of chicken and dumplings to the cellar, with the lid still on it. She wanted to be able to reheat it the following day. The meal had been easier than she'd expected to prepare, but she wouldn't cook it terribly often, so she'd make a lot when she made it.

She noticed Willard was already gone when she got back to the kitchen, but she said nothing as she started doing the dishes. She was angry. Her husband didn't seem to trust her, and he wanted to berate her for someone else's actions. Well, she wasn't going to make it easy for him.

"Francine, the dishes can wait. Talk to me for a minute."

"When the dishes are done." She had never promised to obey him, and he couldn't expect it from her now. She'd told him how it would be. Waiting to do the dishes wasn't something she wanted to do, so she wouldn't do it.

Wally sighed and walked over to help her with the dishes. She'd be done faster with help, and he wanted to get to the talking portion of the evening. Why was she acting so prickly over everything? Had she wanted to leave with the other man?

When the dishes were all done and put away, and she'd wiped down the table and swept under it, she finally sat down with him. She folded her hands in her lap serenely, hoping he wouldn't notice how white her knuckles were. She wanted to scream and throw things at his head for not immediately trusting her, and it was taking everything inside her to act like the lady she'd been raised to be.

"Why was Wally here?"

She shrugged. "He said he wanted to apologize for his bad behavior in New York."

"And did you accept his apology?"

"I've moved on. I told him I didn't need him or his apology."

A slow smile spread across Wally's face. "Of course you did. You're amazing."

She gaped at him for a moment, blinking rapidly. "What did you just say?"

"I said you're amazing. You once thought yourself in love with that man, but you consistently tell him to go away. You're content with where you are in life, and you're doing nothing to try to rekindle an old flame with him."

"Why would I? He married a girl who had made fun of me for years—after impregnating her—all the while escorting me to every function. The man is less to me than a slug, and I want nothing to do with him ever again." She shook her head. "I doubt if his wife and son are dead. They're probably waiting for him to come back to New York, and he thinks he can sweet talk me into his bed. It's not happening. There's only one man I want touching me that way, and it's certainly not him!"

His smile grew. "Oh really? Who do you want touching you that way then?"

She frowned at him. "Only you, and you know it."

"Then come over here and show me." He caught her hand and pulled her onto his lap, his mouth lowering to press his lips to hers. "You're some woman, Mrs. Weston. I think I'm going to keep you."

She wrinkled her nose. "There was a doubt?"

"Not in my mind! You've made me a very happy man, you know."

"Really? Then why did I see doubt on your face when you walked up to the house earlier? You didn't trust that I was true, did you?"

"I did! It was never you I didn't trust. It was him. I can't figure out why he's still here and hasn't gone back to New York where he belongs."

Frankie sighed. "I wish I knew."

"I think we've talked about him enough. I want to work on your Christmas wish."

"My Christmas wish?" She blushed when she realized what he was talking about, running her hands over his shoulders. "I think I can comply with that."

He leaned down and scraped his teeth across the skin on the side of her neck, knowing how she'd respond. "Do we want a boy or a girl first?"

She turned more fully into his arms. "Does it even matter? I plan on having a half dozen of each..."

Chapter Nine

In early December, Frankie couldn't resist going for a walk in the fresh-fallen snow. She loved to go down to the river and see it with the snow all around it. She'd finished all her work for the day except cooking supper, and she had a huge pot of stew on the stove already. Bread was waiting to be put in the oven, so she could serve it still warm with the stew.

As she walked, she dreamed. She could picture herself in five years with three children—a little blond-haired, green-eyed girl like her, a boy with dark hair and brown eyes, and maybe a baby with a dimpled chin. She sighed, liking the picture. In ten years, they could be playing outside during the first snowfall, sledding and building a fort from the snow.

She loved to think of the future of not only her, but the ranch. Someday she knew the ranch would be huge and make people very happy. She didn't know how, but she knew it would happen.

When she returned to the house, she stopped short just before she reached the front step. There, lying on the step, was a single rose. Where had Wally found such a thing? She'd thought they were working all day. She sniffed deeply and took it to put it in a vase in the middle of the table.

She ran water into a vase and stuck the rose in, but when she turned to the table, she saw something else. A jeweler's box, and inside was a pearl necklace. She touched each pearl lightly with the tip of her index finger. How had Wally gotten the money for them? And why hadn't he waited until Christmas to give them to her? That was too big of a gift for just any day!

She would wait until after supper to ask him, because she wanted to be alone with him. Perhaps he'd tell her he loved her. The love she felt for him grew every day, but she had yet to tell him, preferring to wait until he told her first. The necklace was a perfect present to go along with a declaration of love!

Supper was on the table when the men walked in, and Wally dropped a kiss on her lips before turning to wash his hands at the sink.

Frankie put a fresh loaf of bread on the table and sat down across from her brother, her gaze resting on the beautiful rose for a moment. "I thought stew would be nice, because of how cold it is."

Willard smiled, nodding. "You know I always appreciate your stew." He took a huge bite.

Wally's gaze was on the flower. "Where did that rose come from?"

Frankie frowned at him. "You left it on the doorstep for me while I was out walking by the river. It's beautiful. Thank you so much." Why was he pretending it wasn't from him? It had to be!

Wally shook his head slowly. "I was with Willard all day. We were moving the herd to a portion of the land that didn't get quite as much snowfall." They'd also stacked some hay to make windbreaks and put out some extra feed. There was a pond the cattle drank from there, and they had broken the ice. That would be a daily thing until spring.

"But—Who?" As she asked, the answer came to her. Reginald. The man was becoming more than a pest. "You didn't bring me the necklace either, did you?" She suddenly felt as if the thing was alive, and she wanted to tear it off.

"Necklace?" Wally asked, his eyes growing cold. A flower was a lot for another man's wife, but a necklace? That was going too far. Someone needed to do something about Reginald White.

"It was on the table after my walk." She reached behind her neck to unclasp the necklace and hand it to him. "I thought it was from you or I'd have never put it on."

He turned the necklace over in his hand. "It's beautiful."

"I'm sorry," Frankie whispered, embarrassed to have this happen in front of her brother. "I had no idea."

"I'm going to go and have a talk with him. He has no business even staying in Idaho. He's staying at the boarding house in town, and I think it's time he went back to New York." He put the necklace into his pants pocket, planning to take it back and throw it at the other man—if he could resist strangling him with it.

"It's not up to you to talk to him. I'll do it." Frankie took a bite of her stew, her gaze level on his.

"No, I need to deal with this."

"I'll thank you to remember that I spent three years making my own decisions. I don't need a man to watch over me or protect me." How could he have forgotten how strongly she felt about this?

Wally rubbed his hand over the back of his neck, something he only did when he was frustrated. "Willard, will you tell her it's my place to talk to the man?"

"It won't do any good. She's got in her head that she doesn't want you to do it, so if you do, she's only going to be furious."

Wally closed his eyes, counting to ten slowly before he opened them. He should have known his brother-in-law would stay out of it. He'd made it very clear from the very beginning that he was going to stay neutral. "I don't want to fight with you about this, Francine. I want to fight with *him* about this!"

"Don't you dare go into town and speak with him. It's my place to deal with this, and I will deal with it. You will not. Do you hear me?" She got up from the table, making a great deal of noise as she started the dishes.

Willard just kept eating, acting as if nothing was going on around him.

*****

Frankie sat quietly beside her husband and her brother at church two days later. She and Wally had barely spoken since their fight about who should be the one to talk to Reginald. As they were singing, she shared a hymnal with Wally, and she noticed the knuckles of his right hand were bloody. She hadn't been willing to look at him closely enough to notice that the night before.

She looked at his face and saw the corner of his mouth was scabbed over as well. Looking over her shoulder, she spotted Reginald sitting alone at the back of the church, one of his eyes black, and his lip split open and scabbed over. She was shaking she was so angry. "Why?" she hissed at her husband.

He shook his head, refusing to respond to her accusations in church. Of course, her assumption was absolutely correct, and he had come into town the day before and threatened the other man. When his threats hadn't worked, he'd used his fists.

After the service was over, Frankie moved away from her husband and made a beeline for Mary, the widow that ran the boarding house there in town. They had become friends since her marriage to Wally, and she would know exactly who had started the fight between her husband and her former beau.

When Frankie got to Mary, the young woman frowned. She'd only been married a year when her husband had been bitten by a rattlesnake and died, leaving her with only her house to her name. She'd made the most of it and turned her skills for cooking and cleaning into a profitable business, rather than immediately marrying one of the local men who had asked for her hand. She'd told Frankie she needed time to mourn before she could even think of remarrying. "Did Wally seek out Reginald? Or the other way around?"

"I'd like to be able to tell you the fight was started by Mr. White, because I can see from the look on your face that's what you want to hear. But it's not true. Wally came into town yesterday, and he pounded on the front door of my house. When I answered, he walked in past me, and straight into the parlor where Mr. White was sitting. He grabbed him up by his collar and hit him right in the eye. They did some serious damage to my parlor before they were done!"

Frankie sighed. "How much do I owe you for the damages?"

"Mr. White gave me a hundred dollars after the fight was over. He stood staring at the door after Wally had left, and he grinned. I'm happy to say it hurt his lip when he did so! He looked positively gleeful that he'd made your husband mad enough to hit him!"

"Thank you for the information." Frankie was certain one hundred dollars was a great deal more than the damages had come to, so she wasn't worried about that. "I'm very sorry for the fight in your house. I assure you, it will not be happening again."

Mary put her hand on Frankie's arm. "Frankie, don't be so hard on him. He was just trying to get rid of that pesky man."

"I know, but I told him I would handle it. Does he think me incapable of taking care of my own problems? Who does he think fought my fights for me while I spent three years dressed as a man?"

Mary shrugged. "It's in their nature. You can't hold it against him for long."

Frankie hugged her friend, knowing she wouldn't be holding anything against her husband for a while—especially her person. "Thank you for the information. Now I'm going to go home and deal with my husband."

As Mary watched Frankie stalk away, she whispered, "God save him."

*****

Wally watched Frankie the whole way home from church. Willard drove, and Frankie sat between the two men, her hands folded in her lap, and she stared down at her hands demurely. Well, at least it looked like she was staring demurely, but he knew she was really furious, so she was really staring in anger. He sighed.

She didn't even look at him.

"I liked the reverend's message of forgiveness this morning," Willard said to no one in particular. "It's true that people do things that bother us all the time, but if we love them, then we need to forget it happened. 'Love covers a multitude of sins.' Yes, sir, it was a good sermon."

"I thought it was good," Wally said, knowing she was getting angrier with each word spoken. Did Willard not know Frankie at all? He knew his brother-in-law meant well, but really, the words were like putting a bullseye on Wally's forehead.

Frankie sat quietly, and not another word was spoken as they pulled onto the ranch. Frankie had put a pot roast in first thing that morning, so she walked into the house, pulled it from the oven, set the table, and sat down, serving herself.

Willard sat down and served himself as well, watching the married couple carefully. "I think I'm going to spend the afternoon napping in my cabin," he announced before forking up a big bite of meat.

Frankie still hadn't spoken when she'd finished the dishes, and she took her gun and a box of bullets outside. She heard Wally follow her, and that was just fine with her. She couldn't prove her point if he wasn't looking.

She marched out to her practice area, a target painted onto the trunk of one of the tall oak trees on the edge of the property. She efficiently loaded her pistol, cocked it, and held her right hand straight out in front of her, her left hand holding the wrist of the right, before pulling the trigger. A piece of bark from the bullseye jumped off the tree, and she pulled back to cock the gun once more.

Seven times she shot, and seven times she hit her mark. When she was finished, she put her gun into the pocket of her apron and turned to her husband, her arms folded across her chest and a spark of fire in her eye. "Do I shoot as well as you do?"

He nodded. "From what I can see, you shoot as well as any man in the whole country." He'd never seen a woman shoot like that. Heck, he'd never seen a *man* shoot like that!

"Do I seem to you like a woman who would face a man she didn't trust without a weapon?"

"I saw you talking to him with no weapon just a few weeks ago! I know you would talk to him without being armed."

"You saw me talking to him. Did you also see me wearing this apron that day?" Why did he think she was stupid? Because she had breasts, or because she didn't have a penis?

"Well, yes, but you didn't have your gun."

Frankie took a step closer to him. She had to tilt her head way back to be able to see his face, but she had no problem doing that. He had a full foot on her in height, but she backed down from no one. "I had my gun. I was ready for anyone or anything to be at that door. I'm a strong, independent woman, and the next time you treat me like a child, I'll do more than show you I know how to shoot, Wallace Weston! I'll have you know that I am very capable of taking care of myself and everyone around me. I would shoot a man who tried to hurt me or anyone I loved. So you just think about that the next time you decide to go into town and use your fists. I can take care of myself!"

Wally stared after her as she walked away from him, wondering why the fight with her had made him feel so much. He chased after her, catching up with her and grabbing her arm. "I'm sorry, Frankie. I promise I won't do anything that stupid again."

She stood staring at him, feeling the anger slowly leave her body. "Thank you for admitting to your stupidity. Every man should do that."

He couldn't help but grin at the insult. Only his wife could say something like that to him without angering him. "I was stupid. And I might be stupid in some other way again in the future, but I believe in learning from my mistakes. I won't do that particular dumb thing again."

She sighed. "Thank God. I wouldn't want to have to shoot you, but I would!"

He laughed, catching her hips and pulling her close to him. "Have I ever told you that your eyes spark when you get angry, and you look even more beautiful than usual?"

"Have I ever told you that there are days when I want to kick you so hard you'll never walk again?"

He leaned down and pressed his lips to hers. "I'm very impressed at your shooting, Mrs. Weston. We should have a shooting contest sometime."

She smiled, wrapping her arms around his neck. "You know, that would interest me a great deal. You don't cry when you lose, do you?"

"Having so many brothers and sisters taught me to be a gracious winner—and loser. I can do both equally well." He was a crack shot himself, but he wasn't sure that he could outshoot her. "Who taught you to shoot?"

She shrugged. "I told you my mother believed that her daughters should be able to cook, clean, sew, knit, and crochet? My father thought we should be able to protect ourselves. I've been shooting like that since I was thirteen. Don't cross me, Wally Weston."

He knew their crisis was over, because she was calling him Wally again. "I will do my very best."

"See that you do."

Chapter Ten

Two weeks before Christmas, Frankie was sitting at the table carving a special ornament for Wally for their Christmas tree. She'd made one that said, "Our First Christmas 1892" and now she was carving a buck. She knew she had a lot of skills that weren't exactly womanly, but they were useful, and she wasn't going to pretend to be a wilting flower, simply because they might make a man uncomfortable.

Fortunately, Wally seemed to be proud of all of her accomplishments—as long as she wore a dress while practicing them. She loved him more with every passing day, and she knew she was carrying his baby. She was already two weeks late, and she was never late. She was starting to work on another dress that could be let out in the waist later.

She had just finished carving the buck, and was on her way to the bedroom to get some paint to finish it, when there was a knock at the front door. She put her pistol into her apron pocket and opened it, wondering who was there.

"Reginald. Go home."

"Where you are *is* home for me. I'm not going anywhere."

She sighed. "Why don't you understand that I don't want you here?" He had always spoken to her in the same way. It was as if he'd read entire volumes of books on how to woo a woman, and he used everything he'd learned in every conversation. She'd once thought it was romantic, but now she just wanted to shoot him.

"I heard that you got angry with your husband for picking a fight with me. You do care about me, whether you want to admit it or not."

"Do you want to know why I got angry with my husband?" Her voice was deceptively soft for the anger she was feeling. She was quite proud of herself for making it sound that way. Soon, he would realize just how angry she was.

Reginald nodded, his face smug. "Because you still have feelings for me."

She laughed. "No. Because I can take care of myself. I don't need a man hovering over me trying to keep me safe. I can keep myself safe." One day the world would realize that women were just as capable as men were. She couldn't wait for that day to come.

"Just because you dressed as a man for three years doesn't mean you know how to protect yourself."

She shook her head. "No, it doesn't." She pulled the pistol from the apron she wore, and cocked it. "*This* means I know how to take care of myself." She carefully took aim. "I'm going to shoot a branch off the tree hanging over your buggy." His borrowed buggy. If it had been his, she'd have shot the buggy to demonstrate her skill.

He laughed softly. "Sure you are."

She pulled the trigger, a branch falling atop his buggy. "Now, get in your buggy and take yourself right back to New York. If I see you again, I won't be aiming for branches. I'll put a bullet through your shoulder."

He took a step back. "That was a fluke. You didn't hit the branch you were aiming for."

She cocked the pistol again, aiming it straight at him. "It wasn't a fluke. And I've never in my life cocked my gun and not shot it. If you move quickly, this will be the first time." She prayed he would hurry, because she wanted nothing more than to put a bullet through his shoulder. She'd never shot anyone, but at that moment, she wanted to do nothing else.

"Why? You know you love me!" He was slowly backing away as he asked the question.

"Love *you*? I've never loved you! I love my husband!" She watched as he turned and ran for his buggy, sorry to see him go. Moving target practice might be interesting.

"I'm not coming back! If you reject me now, I'll go straight home to New York! Katherine's parents want me to marry her sister."

"As long as you're not in Idaho, I don't care what you do! Get off my property before I shoot you for trespassing."

He drove off quickly, heading for the road. She knew he wouldn't be back. Reginald had always been a bit of a coward, which she'd been willing to overlook at seventeen. At twenty-one, she had no desire to overlook a single one of his flaws. Never again.

*****

Willard froze when he heard the gunshot. "That sounded like it came from the house."

Wally was already running for his horse. They were out checking on the herd, making sure they were all healthy, and they were much too far from the house. He was on his horse and riding home before Willard had time to say another word.

When he reached the house, he threw his leg over the back of the horse, dismounting. Frankie was standing on the front porch, her gun still in her hand. "Frankie? Are you okay? Did someone hurt you?"

Frankie glared at her husband. How long had she stood there, imagining putting a bullet through Reginald? She had no idea, but obviously long enough for him to come back from where he'd been working. "How many times do I have to tell you I can take care of myself? Reginald is gone. I sent him back to New York!" She felt a tear escape her eye then.

"Are you sad that he left? Are you all right?" Why was she crying? Hadn't she wanted Reginald to leave? He couldn't understand what exactly was wrong with her, so he could fix it.

"No, I'm not sad that he left, you fool! I'm sad that I just shouted at him that I love you! I should have told you first, not that lying sack of dung." She knew it wasn't the right way to tell her man she loved him, but when she thought back to his proposal, maybe it wasn't so bad.

Wally walked toward her, carefully removing the pistol from her hand, and putting the safety on. "You love me?" he asked softly, knowing that those words from her would make all his wishes come true.

She nodded. "I do love you. I love you so much." Throwing herself into his arms, she knocked him backward into the snow, landing on top of him and covering his face with kisses.

When Willard rode up to them a moment later, he shook his head. "It's awful cold to be kissing in the snow. You realize you have a bed inside for that kind of thing, right?"

Frankie pulled her mouth away from her husband's for long enough to say, "Go away, big brother. We're kissing here."

"I see that." Willard shook his head and rode off back to the herd. "Wally, take the rest of the day off, would you? I don't want to have to put up with your ugly face anymore today."

Frankie laughed. She rolled to Wally's side and got to her feet, brushing the snow off her dress. There was a great deal more on him than there was on her, so she then helped him brush the snow off of his back, her hands lingering where they would.

She took his hand and led him toward the house, stopping short before opening the door. "You can't come in yet. Give me one minute."

He frowned. "You keeping secrets from me, woman?"

She shook her head. "A week before Christmas is the time to be keeping secrets, don't you think?"

He smiled as she disappeared inside. She was something else. When he'd imagined himself married it was to a petite little woman who said, "Yes, sir," whenever he gave an order. God must have laughed at that when he prayed for a wife. He'd gotten exactly what he needed with Francine.

Frankie hid the ornament in her mending basket and hurried back to the door. She took his hand and pulled him inside. "I'm glad we have a little extra time today, because I want to give you an early Christmas present."

"An early present?" In his family, there had been one present per person, and it was usually something like a pair of socks or mittens. A necessity that was masked as a gift. He'd always been grateful. He knew some of his siblings had wanted toys or frivolities for Christmas, but why? Having warm clothes and enough to eat was all anyone could really ask for.

She nodded, her face glowing. "You'll get other gifts on Christmas morning, of course. But this one—this one is special, and I just can't wait."

"What is it?" he asked, a line between his brows as he drew them together.

She smiled, taking his hand and putting it over her still-flat abdomen. "We're expecting."

His eyes grew wide and he grabbed her, lifting her off her feet and spinning her in a circle. "A baby!"

She laughed happily. "It's the one thing I really wanted, and it's happening. If it's a boy, I want to call him Wilbur. If it's a girl, I want to call her Roberta. Bobbi for short. I've always loved that name!"

"Bobbi?" He wrinkled his nose. "I'm not so sure about naming a girl Bobbi, but Wilbur works. We can call him Will or Willy."

"That works for me!" She sighed contentedly, resting her cheek on his shoulder. "I do love you, Wally."

He cupped her face in his hands, kissing her softly. "I love you with everything inside me, Frankie. I'm glad my sister chose you for me."

She smiled. "Would you have chosen me for yourself?"

He thought about it for a moment before slowly shaking his head. "I don't think I would have. I would have seen you and been afraid of your strength. I would have wanted a woman who would need me to be strong for her, not find her own strength from within."

"But you're happy now?"

He nodded, putting one arm under her knees and scooping her up into his arms, carrying her into the bedroom. "I couldn't be happier. Thank you, Francine Weston, for being what I didn't know I needed."

She sighed, resting her cheek against his shoulder. "Thank you for being willing to let me be who I am and not trying to change me."

Epilogue

Frankie stood between Wally and Willard in front of the tree she had claimed as the Christmas tree. She could see the majestic tree from the window over the sink, and she would look out at it as she cleaned up the dishes from Christmas dinner, smiling at the beauty of it. They were all bundled up, and there was a light snow falling from the sky. It was Christmas Eve, and she handed each of the men a small box.

Willard opened his box and smiled at the small bird she'd carved and painted for the tree. He'd known she would make him one, because she did every year. He reached out and added it to the other six ornaments. One for both of them every year they'd been there. It was something that had mattered to Frankie when they moved there—that they start Christmas traditions for River's End Ranch. Now every year they started out by putting the ornaments from previous years on the tree, and then they added the ones from the current year.

Wally looked at the buck in his hand and turned it over. "This is beautiful. Where did you find this?"

She blushed. "I made it. I wanted you to have your own ornament for our tree."

She pulled the ornament she'd made for herself to hang and placed it on the tree as well. It was the ornament that proclaimed their first Christmas together. Every year she'd make a new ornament for every person that was present. If their new ranch hand, Sebastian, had been there for the holiday, she'd have made him one as well.

"It's our first year all together, and I hope we have many, many more! And Willard needs to find a bride, so she can celebrate with us!" Frankie couldn't believe how excited she was by the idea of having a sister-in-law. "I wish Mary had felt like she could get away to join us. She had to cook Christmas dinner for the boarding house, though."

Willard shook his head. "You wouldn't be trying to marry me off to your new friend, now, would you?"

Frankie shrugged. "Of course I am! I love you both and want you to be happy!"

"And that means we have to marry each other?"

She smiled. "I guess I'm so happy being married, I think everyone should be!"

Rumors from town had said that Reginald was on a train headed east, and Frankie couldn't be happier. She didn't need him around. She needed no one but the ones she loved. She would have the merriest Christmas imaginable. She looked at the tree one last time, the strings of popcorn already drawing birds who were nibbling at it.

Yes, it was a great Christmas.

If you enjoyed this book by Kirsten Osbourne, and want to be notified of new releases, please sign up for her mailing list here[1].

Read on for an excerpt from Rugged Rockclimber by Amelia Adams, book eight in the River's End Ranch series.

1. http://www.kirstenandmorganna.com/newsletter-sign-up

Chapter One

Wesley Weston stepped out onto the front porch of his cabin and took a deep breath of fresh, clean air. There was nothing in the world he loved more than the family ranch near Riston, Idaho, set against the majestic backdrop of mountains so sharp and jagged, they looked like they'd been hewn out of the earth with an ax. He couldn't describe how he felt while he was in the mountains—he just knew that they fed his soul. He'd never tell his siblings that, though—they'd tease him until the day he died. He wasn't supposed to be the deep thinker in the family—that was Wade. Wes was supposed to be the laidback one.

It was nice and bright on this mid-September morning, the perfect weather for some rock climbing. He pulled a crumpled piece of paper from his jeans pocket and checked his schedule. His group of would-be outdoor enthusiasts would be meeting him outside the main house at eleven. A bunch of lawyers, from what Gwen at the front desk had told him when she took the reservation. Sounded like a laugh a minute—he'd need some strong coffee to get him through this one.

He crossed the street and headed toward the diner. Kelsey's Kafè saw far too much of his business—no doubt he'd be having some sort of bypass before he was forty—but he'd blame that on Bob, their new cook. They'd always tried to have a good cook on staff in the past, but Bob had taken everything up a notch, and Wes couldn't help himself because . . . bacon.

"Hey," Kelsi said from behind the cash register when he walked in. "You're five minutes late."

He glanced at the clock that hung on the wall behind her as he took a seat at the counter. "What do you mean? Am I on some kind of schedule?"

"Not a schedule *exactly*, but you've become kind of predictable lately. And let me guess—you want endless strong coffee, bacon and eggs, and two pancakes. Am I right or am I right?"

He opened his mouth to contradict her, but then closed it again. "You're right," he said, conceding defeat.

He watched his sister with amusement as she toddled off to hang up his meal ticket and pour him some coffee. Her softly rounded pregnant belly was just becoming more obvious under her uniform, but she was so excited to be pregnant, she was milking every minute. He swore she added a little extra something to that pregnant waddle, but it wasn't something she did consciously. She just loved the idea of being a mother.

She and her husband, Sheriff Shane Clapper, were going to be excellent parents.

Speaking of parents . . .

"How are the latest additions/renovations coming along?" he asked Kelsi when she handed him his coffee. "Mom and Dad add anything new to the list?"

"Did you hear about the conference center?"

"Yep."

"And the new cabins?"

"Yep. Is there anything else?"

"Not that I know of, but that doesn't mean we're off the hook." She leaned against the counter. "Just be glad they aren't having *you* do anything to improve the place."

"What is there for me to do? I take people rock climbing and hiking. I don't know—maybe I could take them on higher mountains?" He chuckled. "No, I'm perfectly happy just helping the rest of you guys out, thanks. And then, when we finally inherit the place, I'll gladly watch you enjoy your rewards. Just give me my cabin and a cheeseburger once in a while, and I'm good."

"Order up," Bob called out, and Kelsi fetched Wes's plate for him.

Fluffiest pancakes ever. Wes drenched them with syrup, careful to make sure he got some on his bacon too, and went to work.

Dani walked into the diner a minute later and took the seat next to him. She folded her arms on the counter and plopped her head on them, muttering, "Coffee. Lots and lots of coffee."

"Hey, you're in uniform. What's up?" Kelsi asked as she poured her twin sister an extra-large mug.

"Hiker went missing. Search and Rescue got called in around midnight, and we were out all night." Dani lifted her head long enough to gulp down half her cup without adding anything to it. "We finally found him, but that was only because of the dogs. It was too dark to make anything out, and we almost had to call it off until morning."

"Was he all right?" Wes asked.

"He was fine, just cold and hungry. He'd decided to go exploring by himself and got turned around. I just . . . grr." Dani pounded the side of her fist on the counter. "Why can't people get it into their heads? If you're in the woods, don't wander off by yourself. It's . . . it's just common sense. And this guy was from the city and had probably never seen a tree in his whole life. All the more incentive to be careful."

Dani always had been the grumpy twin, but she had a good right to be. Wes knew she'd had to retrieve hikers who hadn't fared nearly so well, and any call for help was reason to be worried. He reached out and gave her left shoulder a super-quick massage. "It's okay. Drink your black stuff and take some deep breaths. You did a good job."

"I won't feel like I've done a good job until people understand that they can't just go off on their own like that. We tell them and tell them and tell them . . ." She sighed and took another swig. "You're right. I need to breathe. I can't keep everyone safe, and stuff happens."

"And they're lucky to have you when it does." Wes finished off his mug and held it up to ask Kelsi for a refill. Why she hadn't given him an extra-large one like Dani's, he didn't know. Maybe Dani got special treatment because she was the twin. "I should probably give you some advance notice that I'm taking a group of lawyers out today. Wouldn't surprise me if one of them got stuck on a rock and we had to call you out."

"One of your clients gets stuck on a rock, that's on you," she replied. "I think part of your job should be to *keep* them from getting stuck."

"True enough." Wes picked up his last piece of bacon and stood up. "I'd better get going—I need to check the equipment before I head out. Listen, Dani, you're amazing. Don't let this get you down, okay?"

She grunted and buried her face in her mug again, and he smiled. She tried so hard to maintain her crusty exterior, but she wasn't nearly as good at it as she thought she was.

"And you take care of my little niece. Or nephew," he called out to Kelsi.

"Oh, I will," Kelsi replied, patting her stomach. "Right now she wants cheese. Lots and lots of cheese."

"So it's a girl today?" Dani asked.

"You know we trade off. Yesterday he was a boy, so today, she's a girl," Kelsi reminded her sister.

Wes grinned and shook his head as he left the diner. This family of his . . .

***

Amber Russell looked around the small engine prop plane at the other lawyers from her firm, trying to ignore the fact that she was off the ground. She'd just been made partner, and Mr. Finnegan had asked all his associates to take this trip as a trust-building exercise to help create unity. She'd done her best to look enthusiastic about the idea while they were in the conference room, but as soon as she'd escaped back into her office, she'd rolled her eyes so hard, they'd almost popped out of her head. A trust-building exercise? Unity? Come on—they were all adults in the professional world. Surely they could run a business together without having to experience the wilds of nature to bring it about.

To her left sat Harold Cramer, a balding forty-nine-year-old with a paunch. While not very impressive in his appearance, he turned into a lion in the courtroom and could reduce anyone to tears and confessions in seconds. His specialty was divorce and family law. Amber felt sorry for anyone who tried to sneak a late child support payment past him.

On the other side of Harold was Giles Green. He was everything Harold wasn't in the looks department. He was tall, blond, muscular, and at thirty-two, closer to Amber's age. He specialized in contract law, and sadly, his personality was just about as dull as the work he did. If Amber could somehow take Harold's personality and go-getter demeanor and Giles's looks and smash them into one guy, she'd create the perfect lawyer. And the perfect man.

There was her mother's voice in her head again. Amber sighed, grateful the noise of the plane allowed her some privacy. She didn't need to find a man in order to be happy . . . she could be happy by herself, no matter what her mother thought. If she *were* to find the right guy, he'd be someone to share her success with, someone to celebrate with—a nice addition to her already fulfilling life. She knew all too well the dangers of believing that someone could "make" her happy. She had to find that within herself, and she had.

The other passenger on the plane was Peter Finnegan, son of Mr. Finnegan. He was the golden child of the firm, no doubt about it. Amber was fairly certain that if he applied at any other firm, he'd never make partner, and yet, here he was, all six feet of entitlement. Mr. Finnegan was a fair employer, but he did have a blind spot when it came to his only offspring. Amber couldn't say that she wouldn't be that way if she ever had children, but seeing the results of it was definitely an object lesson.

The plane began to descend, and the pilot, who had introduced himself as Frank, called over his shoulder, "Landing. If you unbuckled for any reason, make sure you're buckled now."

There hadn't been any reason to unbuckle, so Amber was set to go. Frank brought the plane down on a small landing strip and brought them to a smooth stop, then opened the door and lowered the steps. She stumbled a little bit when her feet touched the tarmac, and Giles reached out and caught her elbow. "Thanks," she said. "I didn't realize I was so off balance."

"Easy to feel some vertigo after a ride on a small plane," Frank explained as he handed her the piece of luggage and the guitar case she'd brought along.

"I'm sure the high heels don't help much either," Harold said.

"They're very helpful," Amber retorted. "I've won some pretty big cases wearing these heels."

"Oh, so that had nothing to do with your lawyering skills and everything to do with the shoes?" Harold gave her a smile, letting her know he was joking.

"The shoes accentuate the skills," she replied, hefting the strap of her bag over her shoulder. She should have treated herself to the rolling luggage she'd seen at the department store the other day, but she just hadn't been able to swallow the price. Now she'd pay that price to someone who'd carry her bag for her.

A short Jeep ride later, they were bouncing through the main gate of River's End Ranch. Amber couldn't take her eyes from the mountains that rose up behind the place. They were even more incredible from the ground than they were from the air—the perspective of looking up at them, of course. She felt dwarfed and insignificant and yet somehow empowered all at the same time. Rumor had it they'd be climbing these mountains. Well, a little hiking never hurt anyone—she was up for the challenge.

The Jeep pulled up right in front of what looked like the main house and came to a stop. Frank hopped out of the driver's seat and made sure that everyone's bags were deposited on the porch, then waved good-bye, saying he had another group to meet. Amber stood with the three other lawyers on the street in front of the building, not really sure what to do next.

"Well, let's check in," Peter said, grabbing his suitcase and walking into the building. There wasn't a bellhop or anything? Amber sighed and picked up her bag and her guitar case again. She was beginning to regret even bringing the instrument along—she doubted she'd have time to play it, but the thought of leaving it behind had seemed wrong somehow, like it would be lonely without her. It was more like, *she'd* be lonely without *it*.

"Welcome to River's End Ranch!" the cute redhead behind the counter said when they filed in. "My name is Gwen, and I'll be your guest services coordinator. Anything you need, just ask, and I'll make sure you have it. Now, you're from the Finnegan firm, right?"

"That's right." Peter stepped forward. "I'm Peter Finnegan. I believe the arrangements were made in my name."

"Yes, they were." Gwen tapped a few keys on her computer. "I have you down for four separate guestrooms here in the bunkhouse, and it looks like your first activity is in an hour. You'll be meeting with our outdoors expert."

"Sounds great," Harold said. "I'm glad we'll have time to change."

"First things first, though—I need each of you to sign this page. It states that you're participating in our activities willingly and lists our qualifications and licensure to be offering these activities to you."

Amber glanced over the form. Standard waiver. Looked pretty straightforward.

Once they'd all returned their papers, Gwen handed them each a keycard. "Here you are. Your rooms are on the second floor. You can take the stairs or the elevator—both are right over there."

Peter headed for the stairs. Of course he would—he always had something to prove. Giles, Harold, and Amber took the elevator like normal people.

The first thing Amber did when she reached her room was to cross the floor and look out the window. She'd never seen anything so green. Spring in Atlanta, where she was from, was certainly beautiful, but September in Idaho had its own kind of beauty, and she pulled in a deep breath.

Her journey to this point had been long and hard. Growing up in Georgia, she'd always wanted to break away from the soft, genteel life her mother had created. Her sister, London, was a little more Southern—she'd gotten involved in charities and beauty pageants and all kinds of other things, but Amber always felt like she was more suited to the boardroom than the parlor. She'd moved to Nashville right after law school, worked as an underling there for two years, then found herself in Oklahoma. It was there that she'd met Mr. Finnegan, and after two years of taking every undesirable case that came the firm's way and proving that she could handle it, she'd been made partner.

She felt old. She wasn't, but she felt that way.

She hefted her bag up on top of the bed and unzipped it. Hiking . . . she'd want some jeans, a T-shirt, and some boots. She'd already owned the clothes, but she'd had to make a run to the store when she learned where they'd be going. She knew it wasn't smart to hike in new shoes, but she'd had no choice, and she'd brought some Band-Aids along as well. Plus, she didn't imagine that Harold would be up for a long day, so she wouldn't suffer too badly.

She changed, then took the time to hang up her clothes and put the rest in the dresser. She'd brought a little of everything, not knowing what else to expect. She was prepared for everything from a light cocktail party to grubbing in the mud. She couldn't picture Peter grubbing, though, so she doubted there'd be much of that. A quick glance at the map of the ranch she'd been given with her keycard told her that yes, there was a pool, so bringing her swimming suit had been a good idea.

And now it was time to join the others. She tugged on her boots and laced them up, grabbed a light jacket and tied it around her waist, just in case, and headed downstairs. It was time to go start trusting each other or whatever.

For the rest of the book, click here[1]! Thank you for reading!

Yes, it was a great Christmas.

1. https://www.amazon.com/Rugged-Rockclimber-Rivers-Ranch-Book-ebook/dp/B01MT0P0SE/ref=sr_1_1?s=digital-text&ie=UTF8&qid=1482894882&sr=1-1&keywords=rugged+rockclimber

Milton Keynes UK
Ingram Content Group UK Ltd.
UKHW011816011223
433620UK00001B/91

9 798223 064411